Drew put his arm around her shoulders. 'It  **you. If there is to help, you onl**

She looked up at hi tempted by his nearness. she saw that her brother had come through the swing doors and was walking towards her. She was alarmed in case he had witnessed their brief embrace. She couldn't help herself. Her instant reaction was to stiffen and draw back from Drew.

It was hard working with Drew, getting to know him all over again and feeling the tug of her emotions pull her in all directions. How could she allow herself to lean on him and accept his support when her family was so antagonistic towards him…?

When **Joanna Neil** discovered Mills & Boon®, her life-long addiction to reading crystallised into an exciting new career writing Medical Romance™. Her characters are probably the outcome of her varied lifestyle, which includes working as a clerk, typist, nurse and infant teacher. She enjoys dressmaking and cooking at her Leicestershire home. Her family includes a husband, son and daughter, an exuberant yellow Labrador and two slightly crazed cockatiels. She currently works with a team of tutors at her local education centre to provide creative writing workshops for people interested in exploring their own writing ambitions.

Recent titles by the same author:

THE CONSULTANT'S SECRET SON
HER CONSULTANT KNIGHT
CHALLENGING DR CARLISLE
THE DOCTOR'S FAMILY SECRET
A CONSULTANT'S SPECIAL CARE

EMERGENCY
AT THE ROYAL

BY
JOANNA NEIL

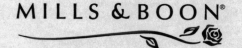

MILLS & BOON®

*First published in Great Britain 2005
Harlequin Mills & Boon Limited,
Eton House, 18-24 Paradise Road, Richmond, Surrey TW9 1SR*

© Joanna Neil 2005

ISBN 0 263 84313 0

*Set in Times Roman 10½ on 12½ pt.
03-0605-44358*

*Printed and bound in Spain
by Litografia Rosés, S.A., Barcelona*

CHAPTER ONE

'SOMETHING must be really wrong. Do you see that van driver? What's he doing?'

Oblivious to everything around her, Katie had been sipping her coffee in a peaceful corner of the café, but now, hearing a quiet buzz of conversation, she looked up and glanced around. Who had said that? She couldn't be sure, but she was conscious of a slight disturbance starting up around her, of a faint hum of distracted chatter passing through the room.

Her mind had been somewhere else—sitting here was the perfect chance to enjoy a few moments of relaxation after her afternoon shopping trip. Would Reece like the wooden train set she had bought for him? Thinking about her brother's little boy, she smiled. He would be four years old next week, and he loved to play with anything that had wheels, so with luck he would appreciate her birthday gift.

'Oh, no. Look at him—he's all over the place.'

Katie was startled into attentiveness once more. Lost in her own thoughts, she had missed what was going on. Now, though, she realised that people were getting up from their tables and going over to the window.

'What's he doing? He's lost control—oh, those poor people.'

Katie put her cup down on its saucer and turned towards the window to see what everyone was looking at, and a nightmare image met her eyes. Across the street, a van was mounting the pavement, and people who had been in its path were scattering in sheer panic. Then the vehicle smashed into a wall and came to an abrupt halt.

Katie didn't stop to think any longer. She was on her feet in an instant and running out of the café towards the wreck of the van and the devastation of shattered brickwork and damaged people who simply hadn't managed to escape in time.

Assessing the full horror of what had happened, she pulled in a deep breath and her mind flipped smoothly into professional mode. Her phone was in her handbag, and she reached for it now and called for an ambulance.

As she spoke, her gaze flicked along the street and she saw that a passing car was slowing down. She guessed that the driver was about to pull in at the side of the road. Other drivers seemed to be following suit, and a small crowd was beginning to gather.

As far as Katie could see, there were four casualties—the van driver, who was slumped across his steering-wheel, a man who was sitting crumpled on the pavement and next to him a woman who was crying out in shock and despair. Finally, there was a small child who was lying on the ground to one side of the front of the van.

'Help us, please,' the woman said, tears rolling down her cheeks. 'My little boy—he's not moving. I don't know what to do.' Her voice cracked. 'How could this be happening to us?' Her blonde hair was damp and streaked with blood, and she was shaking, her face white with anguish.

'I'm a doctor,' Katie said, gently. 'I'll do what I can. Try to stay calm while I check everyone out.'

She could see that the woman was bleeding from a head wound and that her arm was grazed, but at least she was breathing and talking, and Katie wasn't worried about her for the moment. The man was nursing his abdomen, but he, too, was conscious, and Katie turned her attention to the child.

He was about six years old, and he was lying very still, but his eyes were open, and she said softly, 'Hello. I'm Katie. Can you tell me your name?'

'Matthew.' He forced the word out between his lips.

'Can you tell me where it hurts, Matthew?'

'It's my leg.' His eyes blazed in sudden warning. 'Don't you touch it.'

'All right, Matthew. I'll be very careful, I promise.' She examined him briefly, and then said, 'I'm going to leave you for a moment while I go and take a look at the other people who are hurt. I'll be back very soon. Your mum will sit with you, and you're going to be all right, so don't worry.'

She glanced up at his mother, who was by his side, and the woman reached for his hand and clasped it to her chest. 'My husband,' she said in a thready voice. 'He's in terrible pain.'

'I know. I'll go and look at him now.'

She discovered that the woman's husband had some broken ribs and an abdominal injury. 'I'll come back to you in just a moment,' she told him. 'I have to go and see who else is injured.' Her priority was to treat the person with the most serious injuries first, and she hoped he understood that. He nodded almost imperceptibly.

'Take care of my little boy. I couldn't bear it if anything happened to him.'

'I will. I'll see to him as soon as possible.'

She climbed up into the cab of the van, accessing it from the side that was still intact. The driver made a mumbled, incoherent response when Katie spoke to him, and when she checked him over she discovered that his reflexes were poor and that his limbs were weak on one side. He was in a very bad way and she was concerned about his condition, but she was worried about the others, too. All of these people needed help urgently, but she was only one person, and she had to deal with the most seriously injured first.

As she twisted around in the cab of the van, she saw that a man was approaching. Was he going to be able to help her? From her position, peering downwards, all she could see was a pair of long legs encased in crisp chinos. His stride was brisk and purposeful, and as she glanced up she saw that he was wearing a dark blue shirt made of good-quality linen.

He said briskly, 'Can I do anything to help?' His voice was deep and firm, easy on the senses.

'I hope so.' Katie looked at him properly then, and her mouth dropped open a little in sudden recognition. He had night-black hair, cut short in an attractive, stylish manner, and his features were strong and bone-meltingly familiar. His blue-grey eyes met hers steadily, and after a moment she realised that she was staring. She recovered herself quickly, clamping her lips together in an attempt at control.

'Drew?'

What was he doing here? How many years had it been since she had last seen him? She didn't stop to voice her thoughts, though. This was no time to start asking questions, and instead she made an effort to pull herself together and concentrate her attention on her patients.

'Katie. It's not the best circumstance for us to meet up again, is it?' His mouth made an odd, rueful shape. 'I was driving through town and I saw what happened. Have you checked everyone?'

She nodded. 'I think the driver must have had a stroke of some kind. The ambulance is on its way. He needs oxygen and we need to get him to hospital fast.'

She noticed that Drew had his medical bag with him. He saw her glance and said evenly, 'I keep it in the car for emergencies, along with other things that

I might need. I can grab whatever else we might want from the boot. I'll start by giving him oxygen and I'll set up an IV line.'

'Good. I'll go and see to the others. I think the little boy has a fractured femur. He's probably bleeding internally and he'll need fluids and something for the pain. I'll secure the leg with tape and padding to make sure there's no further damage.'

'Help yourself to whatever you need. What about the man on the pavement? Have you examined him?'

'Only very briefly. He has an abdominal injury, broken ribs and possibly a ruptured spleen, so I'll give him replacement fluids, too. We'll need to notify the surgeon to be prepared. The woman was lucky. She seems to have escaped with cuts and bruises.'

'Shout if you need me.' Drew was already turning away to minister to the van driver.

'I will.' She hurried away to tend to the child and his father. She was still overwhelmed by the shock of seeing Drew here, out of the blue, and as if the suddenness of the accident hadn't been enough to make her adrenaline surge, the mere fact of his presence had sent her pulse into overdrive.

She was confused and edgy because of his unexpected arrival, but she was glad that he was by her side in this. He was resourceful and skilled, and the perfect man to have around in a crisis. She just couldn't get used to the idea that he was here in Devon at all. The last she had heard of him was that he had taken the job of A and E consultant in the north of the country.

The sound of an ambulance siren came to her as she was taping the IV line in place on the little boy. She had covered him with her jacket to keep him warm, and the painkilling injection she had given him was beginning to do its work.

'Who's in charge here?' the paramedic asked, looking from Katie to Drew.

'I am,' she answered, and filled him in on details of the condition of each patient. 'The man on the pavement and the boy will need to be taken to A and E. I think the van driver has suffered a stroke, so the stroke unit should be contacted as soon as possible. As for the woman, she's in shock, and has a head wound, so she also needs to be looked at more closely. But I believe all but the stroke victim are stable for the moment. Shall I come with you to the hospital?'

He shook his head. 'You don't need to do that. It looks as though you've done everything possible for them, and we'll manage the rest. It's only a few minutes' drive from here after all. Thanks for your help.'

'You're welcome.' Katie stood back and watched as the patients were transferred to the ambulance. Drew came and positioned himself next to her, his arm accidentally brushing hers, and her body reacted like quicksilver, as though he had lit a fuse in her.

Nothing had changed. She had always responded to him this way, and it seemed as though the intervening years had done nothing to extinguish the instant flame that seared her flesh and made her heart pound whenever he was close.

She had hoped that time would change the way she felt about him, but now she accepted that was a vain hope. All those feelings had come rushing back in full force, along with the memory of how their relationship had abruptly ended. There could never be any going back.

She shifted away from him, just a fraction, so that there was no possibility of him touching her any more, and she tried hard to control her breathing, until it was a little more calm and even and no longer coming in quick spurts.

She remembered the last time she had seen him, when he had been moving on to begin his specialist training. How long ago had that been...seven, eight years? That had been when she had been just eighteen and she had been getting ready to go to medical school to prepare for her own career. It hadn't been a happy time for her back then. Harsh words had been said on both sides when they had parted, and she knew that things could never be the same between them.

'You must have qualified as a doctor, then? Are you specialising in A and E?' he asked, his glance flicking over her.

She nodded.

'I imagine you would have done very well,' he murmured, 'because I thought you handled the situation here with great skill and expertise. It would have been daunting for anyone, but you were exceptionally cool and organised. It was impressive.'

Her smile was strained. 'I can't say that I felt that way. I didn't have time to stop and think or I might have been even less sure of myself. I was worried about the little boy. He looked so helpless lying there, so young and vulnerable, but I knew I had to attend to the driver first. His condition was the worst.'

'They're all safe now, thanks to you.'

She made a face. 'Thanks to your medical equipment, more like. I think I shall have to start carrying emergency supplies with me, just in case.'

'It helps to be prepared for anything.' He looked at her thoughtfully. 'Are you working locally?'

'Yes. I've just finished my senior house officer year, and now I'm working in A and E at the Royal. It's a bit daunting, because there have been some staff changes lately, with promotions and people moving on, but I'm glad to be able to work in a place that I'm familiar with.'

She sent him a quick glance. 'I hadn't expected to see you again. What are you doing in this neck of the woods? I heard on the grapevine that you were working as a consultant up north.'

'That's true. I've been running my own department for a couple of years now.'

'That was what you always wanted, wasn't it?' Her

mouth moved in an odd shape. 'I thought you would do well for yourself. You worked hard and you were very determined.'

She had never known him to fail at anything. 'You still haven't told me what you're doing down here. You're a long way from home.'

'Not really. My family still live hereabouts. In fact, I was passing through on my way to a meeting.' He grimaced and glanced at his watch, and as he lifted his arm she saw that his wrist was faintly bronzed by the sun and was covered by a smattering of dark hairs. His hands were strong and capable, and now her breath caught in her throat as she remembered the way those hands had once gently caressed her.

She looked away. That was all over now, finished. 'Will you be too late for your meeting now?'

'Maybe not. I'll be a bit late, but that can't be helped.' He studied her features. 'You haven't changed a bit.'

'Haven't I? I feel as though I'm a lot older and wiser.'

He smiled. 'Maybe, but you still look the same. Your hair is still glorious and untamed and glowing like fire. I always thought there was such a contrast between that fiery auburn and the calmness of your eyes. They're such a soft, peaceful green.'

'They don't necessarily reflect how I feel.' She watched the ambulance pull away and hoped that the people inside would be all right. There was nothing more that she could do for them.

'I should go now,' she said. His words had unsettled her, made her think of things that could not be. He was just passing through, and even if that hadn't been the case she couldn't have stayed with him and chatted as though all was well. Things would always be fraught between them. 'Time's getting on and there are some things I need to do.'

'Is your car nearby?'

She nodded, and he said, 'I'll walk with you to it.'

'If you like.' She was feeling a little shaky after the events of the afternoon, and for all her conflicting emotions it wouldn't do any harm to have him accompany her for a bit longer, would it? She turned and began to head towards the parking bay.

'Do you still live with your family in the old farmhouse?' he asked.

She shook her head. His question troubled her. Didn't he know that they had been forced to sell the house? 'I decided that I needed a place of my own. The farm cottage came up for sale a couple of years ago, and it seemed just about the right size for me, so I snapped it up when I had the chance.'

'The one near to your family home?'

She nodded. 'That's right. It isn't the family home any longer, though. My parents moved away and bought a smaller place near the sea.'

He frowned. 'I hadn't realised that. I thought the house had been in your family for some generations. It was a beautiful old place and they loved it, didn't they? I didn't think they would ever want to move.'

'They decided to go for something more manageable.' It hurt to remember that the family home had been sold. No one had wanted to see it go, and even though it had been put on the market again recently by its new owners, there was no chance that they would be able to buy it back. It would cost far more than they could afford.

There wasn't any point in telling Drew what had really happened, that they had been left with no choice but to sell. It would only serve to rake up old wounds and it was highly unlikely that she would be seeing see him again after today.

'How is your father these days?' he said. 'I was worried about him. His health was never good, was it? And I know he took a turn for the worse just before I left.'

Her mouth made a bitter line. 'What did you expect? As you said, he was ill to begin with and what happened came as a complete shock to him. He built his business up from nothing, and then your father came along and took it from him and everything he'd worked for was destroyed. It was bound to make him ill.'

'I don't think that's fair. It wasn't my father's fault. By the time he came along your father had already opened his company up to shareholders. They were the ones who made the decision to sell out.'

'It was your father's board of directors that voted him out after the new company took over. My dad hadn't been prepared for that to happen. It was a hostile take-over from start to finish. He founded the business and in the end he was left with nothing. Everything he'd worked for his whole life was taken from him.'

'He was well compensated. He didn't walk away with empty hands.'

She glared at him, her green eyes flashing contempt. 'Do you think money is all that matters? His health was so bad afterwards that for a long time he couldn't work. He was a broken man, and it took him a long time to recover, and when he was well enough he had to start again from nothing.'

Drew stopped walking and reached for her, grasping her shoulders in a gentle but firm embrace. He made her look at him and she was so taken aback that she forgot to struggle, and the warmth of his palms seeped through her thin cotton top and heated her flesh and took her breath away.

'Katie, I'm sure my father didn't mean for any of that to happen. He acted in the best interests of his company, as any businessman would. He didn't intend to hurt anyone.'

'Didn't he? My father wasn't the only one to suffer, was he? The workers were laid off, too. They weren't prepared for the new owners to simply asset-strip and then move on.'

She shrugged off his hands and moved towards her car. Drew could still see nothing wrong in what happened. All those years ago, people had said to her that he was like his father, ruthless and ambitious, but she hadn't wanted to believe them. Was it true after all? Why couldn't he see the way her father had been hurt?

He watched her unlock her car door. 'Katie,' he said quietly, 'all of this happened a long time ago, and it was a dispute between our parents, not the two of us. There's no reason why you and I can't still be friends, is there?'

'I have to be loyal to my family,' she said. 'I'm surprised that you can't see that.'

'Of course I see it. It doesn't stop me from believing that we can at least try to put all the bad feelings behind us.'

'I don't think my family see it that way. Even after all this time they're still suffering the effects. For us, it doesn't stop.'

'I'm sorry. I know it must be difficult for you, but I thought that as we had met up again we could at least spend some time together. I'll be in the area for a day or two and I wondered if we might have dinner together, or maybe just a coffee.'

'I don't think that's going to be possible. You have your meeting to go to, and I have to work over the next few days.' She sent him a quick, troubled glance. 'I am glad that we met up again, though,' she said in a mollified tone, 'and I really appreciate all your help this afternoon. I don't know what I would have done if you hadn't been there.'

He made a wry smile. 'I'm sure you would have managed very well.'

She pulled open her car door and he rested his hand
on the rim of it. 'Are you sure that I can't persuade
you to change your mind?'

'I'm sure. I can't,' she said, and she was conscious
of a tremor in her voice. She hoped he hadn't noticed
it, too. 'I must go. I have to get to the pharmacy
before it closes. I promised that I would collect my
father's prescription since I'm in town.'

'All right. I'll let you go.' He made a rueful smile.
'Perhaps we'll meet up again soon.'

'Perhaps,' she said, but she knew that they
wouldn't. She put her key in the ignition, and as soon
as he had released the door she pulled it shut and
started the engine. As she drove away, she glanced in
her rear-view mirror and saw that he was still standing
there, watching her go.

She completed her errands and then drove to her
parents' home. Letting herself in through the kitchen
door, she saw that her brother was there.

'Katie…you're here at last. Thank heaven for that.
I was beginning to worry.'

Katie looked at her brother and frowned. She
hadn't expected to be pounced on the moment she
walked into the room.

'Why? What's wrong? I'm not all that late.' She
slipped her jacket over the back of a chair and laid
her handbag down on the pine table. 'I've been to the
pharmacy for Dad's medication. Mum asked me to
collect it on my way home.'

Luke looked faintly dishevelled, his black hair

awry, as though he had been running his fingers through it, and his grey eyes were troubled. She asked quietly, 'Is something wrong with Dad?'

'He's not too well. I wasn't sure what to do. I wanted to phone for the doctor, but Mum said she was expecting you.'

Katie was anxious all at once. 'Why didn't you ring me—you know my mobile number, don't you?'

'Yes, but Mum thought you would be driving, and she stopped me.'

'Where is he?'

'In the living room. He had a funny turn and couldn't get his breath.'

Katie was already heading that way. 'Do you know what started it? What was he doing before he started to be ill?'

'He wasn't doing anything. We were talking about the business and I was telling him that I've been trying to get some new contracts.' He sent her a guilty look. 'I'm probably to blame. I shouldn't have gone on about things, but it hasn't been easy lately, trying to keep everything running smoothly, and I think he feels that he should be doing more to help out. He can't, of course, and that makes him frustrated. That last bout of bronchitis must have taken more out of him than he realised.'

Katie pushed open the living-room door and glanced around. Her father was sitting in an armchair, looking pale and trying to disguise the fact that he was in pain.

Her mother was by his side, but she turned as Katie approached and gave her a swift, weak smile. 'Katie,' she said, 'your dad's not feeling very well. Can you do anything to help him?'

Katie knelt down beside her father. 'Luke says you're a bit breathless,' she said. 'Are you having any chest pain?'

Her father patted her hand. 'Your mum and Luke both worry too much,' he said in a wheezy voice. 'I'll be fine in a little while. I just need to rest for a bit.'

'Let me just feel your pulse and check you over,' she murmured, and he gave a faint nod and leaned his head back in the chair.

After a moment or two she said quietly, 'I think you're having another of your angina attacks. They seem to be coming on a bit more often these days, don't they? Have you taken your medication?'

He nodded again, and her mother said quickly, 'It didn't seem to work very well. I told him he should go and see his doctor and tell him that he hasn't been feeling too good lately, but you know how stubborn he is.'

Katie smiled. 'Yes, I do know that.' She clasped her father's hand. 'I think you need a painkiller, and another one of your tablets, just to calm things down. Mum's right. You really should go back to your GP and get him to refer you back to the specialist.'

She went and fetched some tablets from the medicine cupboard, and gave them to her father with a glass of water. 'Do you think you'll be all right while

Mum and I go and make you a cup of tea?' she asked after a minute or two. 'It might help to make you feel a bit better.'

'I'll be fine. Anyway, Luke's going to sit and talk to me, aren't you, Luke?'

Her brother nodded, and Katie gave him and her father a warning look. 'There's to be no talk about business. Am I making myself clear?'

Both men nodded, looking sheepish, and Katie went off to the kitchen to put the kettle on.

'Luke was anxious about him,' her mother said, following her in there. 'He was getting quite agitated even though you were just a few minutes late. I think he's finding it a strain, managing the business on his own.'

Katie helped to set the cups out on a tray. 'Luke never expected to be running the business and concentrating on administration, did he? He had other things in mind when he left university—he always preferred the design engineering side of things—but he couldn't just stand by and see Dad struggle. You have to give him his due…he made sure that he did the right thing.'

Her mother made a face. 'Well, let's face it, nothing has gone the way it should ever since Jacob Bradley took over Sherbourn Medical Equipment. It doesn't even have your father's name any more, and the last I heard, Bradley wasn't with the company. He just took what he wanted and moved on.' She was silent for a moment, musing on things. 'I wonder what happened to him and his family?'

Katie hesitated, wondering if she should say anything about her meeting with Jacob's son. Perhaps it would be better coming from her than from another source, though. Someone might have seen them together. She poured milk into a jug, and then said cautiously, 'I saw Drew Bradley this afternoon.'

Amy Sherbourn stopped what she was doing and looked at Katie. She appeared shocked, her face pale against the dark auburn of her hair. 'How did that come about? I hope that doesn't mean the family are going to be close by.'

'I don't think so, though they still live in the area. I don't suppose we'll run into them.' She couldn't be sure, though, and it was probably better that it was out in the open. At least this way her mother would be able to prepare her dad for anything unforeseen. 'We both stopped to help out at the scene of an accident.' Katie told her mother what had happened that afternoon.

As she was speaking, Luke appeared at the kitchen door. 'You're saying that he's back?' he said, sounding incredulous. 'I heard something of what you were saying to Mum. I can hardly believe it.'

Katie swung around to look at him properly. 'He's only here for a short time, as far as I know,' she said, 'and it doesn't necessarily mean that his family are going to be moving closer.' She studied his face briefly. 'Is Dad all right?'

'He's OK. I think the painkiller must have begun to kick in. He asked me to find out what's happening with the tea.'

'That sounds as though he's feeling better.' She poured the tea and set some biscuits out on a plate on the tray. 'It's ready. You can take it in to him.'

Luke's mouth set in a taut line. 'Drew was every bit as bad as his father. He wouldn't hear anything wrong about him. None of them cared that we lost everything, including the house.'

'I don't think they realised that happened,' she said, 'and you can't hold Drew responsible for what his father did.'

'No, but he's like him in a lot of ways. Not that you could ever see it. You've always been ready to stand up for him. He could never do anything wrong in your eyes, could he? You were sweet on him.'

'That was a long time ago. What happened affected me badly, too, you know. I didn't like what happened either, and it hurt me as well when we had to sell the house.'

Luke winced. 'I'm sorry. I didn't mean to go on at you. It was just hearing that he's back that set me off. In my head he's tarred with the same brush as his father. Anyway, I expect he'll go away again, like he did before. He didn't bother to make any contact then, did he? You'd have thought he would if he had cared about you.'

Katie flinched. 'I'm sure he had his reasons. Anyway, we parted on bad terms after what happened. I don't imagine he would have wanted to meet up with any of us after that.' Luke's bitterness stemmed from having to stand in for their father and take over the family business, and it was understandable that he felt the way he did.

As for herself, it had hurt that Drew had gone away, and when she had recovered from the initial sting of bad feeling she had inwardly hoped that he would get in touch. He hadn't, though, and she had got on with her life and tried to put him out of her mind.

Now, in the space of a few short hours, all those emotions had been stirred up once again, and she felt the heartache every bit as much she had before. The repercussions of the dispute between their families went on and on.

CHAPTER TWO

AT LEAST her father was feeling better by the time Katie left her parents' house. She was still worrying about him, though, as she made her way to her own cottage.

It was getting late by now, and there were chores she had to finish before her time was her own, but that wasn't such a bad thing. If she kept busy it would help her to work through her frustrations. So far it had been a peculiar day, one way and another, and she was feeling edgy and distracted.

The house was small and cosy, just right for her, and it wouldn't take her long to tidy up all the things she hadn't had time to sort out that morning. As soon as she had done that, she would turn her thoughts to her evening meal. Her mother had offered to cook for her, but she had been too uptight to eat just then. Luke's bitter recriminations had upset her.

The doorbell suddenly rang, startling her as she was folding away the last few items of clothing in the airing cupboard. Who could that be?

She went downstairs to investigate, and when she opened the door and saw Drew standing in the porch she let out a little gasp of astonishment.

She said awkwardly, 'I hadn't expected to see you again...at least, not quite so soon.'

He lifted a dark brow and his mouth made an odd quirk. 'I hope that doesn't mean you're going to turn me away?'

She recovered herself and stood back from the door. 'No, of course not. I don't know what I was thinking.' She couldn't leave him standing on the doorstep, and so she waved a hand towards the end of the short hallway. 'Come in. Do you want to come through to the kitchen? I was just about to make a pot of coffee.'

He followed her into the room and glanced around. She said defensively, 'It's only tiny, but it does for me. I haven't been here long, just a few months, and there are still things I need to put right. I've done a bit of decorating and changed the floor tiles, but it isn't quite as I want it yet.' She was babbling, nervousness getting the better of her, and she clamped her mouth shut. Why was she defending her home to him?

'I think it's lovely,' he murmured. 'You chose well with the pale yellow for the walls, and everything looks bright and cheerful in here. I like the way you've found room for a breakfast bar in the corner.' He sent her a quick, easy smile. 'That is one of your touches, isn't it? I recognise the style.'

She had done something similar in the old family house, renovating the kitchen in an attempt to make it light and cheery. 'That's right,' she said. 'I'm surprised that you remember.'

She turned away to set up the coffee-percolator. She felt awkward, talking to him as though the years that had gone by had dissolved into nothingness, and she still had no idea what he was doing there.

Perhaps he sensed her discomfort, because he said, 'I brought your shopping bag. Someone handed it to me when I walked back towards my car this afternoon. You left it in the café apparently, and the woman who gave it to me had seen us talking together and guessed that we knew each other. She asked me if I would pass it on to you.'

'Oh, heavens…' She stared at the bag in dismay. 'I'd forgotten all about it.' She glanced up at him. 'Thank you for taking the time to bring it to me.'

'It was no trouble. With everything that went on, I'm not surprised that you forgot it. I'm just glad that you told me where you were living so that I was able to bring it to you.' He set the bag down on a clear space on the worktop. 'I couldn't get it to you any earlier. My meeting went on for much longer than I expected.'

She glanced at the contents of the bag. 'Thanks again,' she said, relieved. 'I'm so glad to have it back. I was just so worried about those poor people that I wasn't thinking properly when I rushed out of the café.' She paused, remembering what had happened. 'I hope they're all right.'

'I rang the A and E department to check up, and

the consensus was that they seem to be doing as well as can be expected. The man and the boy both had surgery and came through it all right, and the van driver has been transferred to the stroke unit. He's lost the movement in an arm and leg, but they're hoping he'll regain that in time, after intensive therapy.'

'That's good to hear.' She studied him briefly, her gaze running over his strong features, taking in the straight line of his jaw and his firmly moulded mouth. He was far too good-looking for her peace of mind, and she had to get a grip on herself before she spoke again. 'It was thoughtful of you to follow it up. I didn't expect to find out what had happened to them until I got in to work in the morning.'

She might have known he would check up. He wasn't one to leave loose ends. Even after the row that had erupted between her family and his, he had made his position clear. He had stood by his father, and he believed her father had been well compensated for his loss. She had never been able to come to terms with that, and it had coloured everything between them after that. Now that he had turned up again she was at war with herself, and her emotions were all over the place.

What was she to make of him? Her brother thought he was tough and ambitious, unyielding in his attitude, and yet Drew had shown her a caring side, a concern for the well-being of others. Wasn't that why he had become a doctor?

She couldn't make any sense of her feelings towards him. She was confused, drawn to him on the one hand but wary on the other, and all the time she was conscious of the way her brother and her parents felt about him and his family.

She glanced at him once more. He looked weary, a faint shadow of tiredness around his eyes, and she guessed it had been a long day for him. 'Do you want to sit down?' she asked. 'I'll just finish making the coffee. Have you eaten?'

He shook his head. 'I didn't get the chance.' He pulled out a bar stool and angled himself on it by the breakfast corner. 'I was hoping to grab some lunch before my meeting, but that all changed, as you know.'

'I'll heat some pasties,' she offered, 'and I've a bowl of salad to go with them. Not the most adventurous of meals, but it might fill a gap.' He had taken the trouble to bring her shopping bag to her, and it was the least she could do to return the favour.

She watched him guardedly. She still couldn't get used to the idea that he was here at all, and there was no point in wondering about what was to come of it. He would soon be moving on and out of her life once more.

As they ate, he said lightly, 'I couldn't help noticing that your shopping was mainly toys. A wooden train set and some baby things.' He gave her a quizzical look. 'Is there something I don't know about? Are you married now? What have you done with the children? I don't see them around, or maybe they're in bed?'

She gave him a brief, taut smile. He didn't seem at all concerned by the idea that she might be a mother, and for some reason that bothered her.

'No, I haven't married…yet. The train set is for my brother's little boy, Reece, and the baby clothes are for the baby he and his wife are expecting. I thought I would get things in neutral colours since they don't know whether they're going to have a boy or a girl. They were in a sale, so I took the opportunity to buy now.' She gave a small frown. 'Perhaps I shouldn't have—I'm way ahead of myself.'

'Is there a problem with being prepared?' His blue-grey eyes watched her curiously.

'No…not really, but Becky hasn't been feeling too well through this pregnancy. I hope I'm not jumping the gun.'

'Is there any particular reason why she's unwell?'

'I'm not sure.' She frowned again. 'Things have been difficult for Becky and Luke this last few months and she might be suffering under the strain. Luke is trying to cope with running Dad's business, and it's been quite stressful for him lately. My dad's been able to do less and less, and Luke's finding it hard to manage on his own.'

'Can't he bring in more people to help out?'

'I suppose he could, but that would mean training them up, and anyway I'm not sure that the business is doing well enough for them to take on more staff.

Drew's done his best these last few years to make a success of things, but working in management was never part of his plan when he left university.'

'It's difficult, I know, but sometimes things don't go the way we want them to.' He didn't look particularly concerned. 'I'm sorry to hear that your dad is still having problems with his health. Is there anything that can be done to improve things for him?'

'Possibly. I've persuaded him that he needs to go and see the specialist again.' She glanced at Drew's plate, and saw that he had finished his food. 'Can I get anything more for you? I think there's some more crusty bread if you want it.'

'No, thanks. That was good, but I must be on my way now.' He pushed back his chair and stood up. 'Thanks again for the food,' he said. 'It filled me up and made me feel much more human.' He gave her a fleeting smile. 'Perhaps we'll meet up again some time.'

'Maybe.' She didn't believe that was true, but it was easier to say it and to see him out. She went with him to the door and watched him climb into his sleek silver saloon car. Part of her wanted to beg him to stay, but her innate sense of self-preservation held her back. He drove away without looking behind him and she felt as though the lifeblood was draining out of her. She was empty inside.

A few days later, in A and E, she took advantage of a few minutes' break to wind down. She had been on the go all morning, and when there was a slight lull, she stopped by the desk and chatted to Craig, a senior house officer who had been spending the last six months learning about emergency medicine.

'How's things?' he asked. 'I didn't see you at the party last weekend. I was hoping you might be able to pop in for an hour or so.'

'Something came up,' she said. 'I heard that you had a good time. Something about dancing the conga through the park?'

He laughed. 'We all had a bit too much to drink.' He leaned a little closer and slid an arm around her waist. 'It would have been so much better if you had been there.'

She smiled at him. 'You're an inveterate flirt,' she said.

'You can't blame a man for trying. One of these days you might agree to come out with me.'

'In your dreams.' Craig would have been a catch for any young woman, with his dark good looks and happy-go-lucky attitude, but Katie was steering clear of any kind of commitment. He was far too casual in his relationships for her to take him seriously and, anyway, she was looking for something more in a man, something that remained elusive. There had only been one love of her life, and that had turned to ashes. She wasn't about to let herself get burned again.

An ambulance siren sounded in the distance, and she readied herself to receive her next patient. Craig went off humming to himself, full of beans, and she heard him call the name of a man who was in the waiting room. She had no idea how he could be so lively at this time of the day. Katie glanced at his patient. He looked as though he was hurting, but she couldn't see any particular injury.

Her own patient was suffering from a particularly nasty fracture, and she called on Hannah to assist her. Hannah was an A and E nurse, with many years of experience of working in Emergency, and Katie liked working with her.

'Have you seen the new consultant?' Hannah asked.

Katie lifted a brow. 'No—I didn't know he was about. I've been so busy today I've been chasing my own shadow. What's he like?' She made sure that her patient had a painkilling injection and called for a surgical consultation.

'He's incredible.' Hannah lifted her eyes heaven-wards. 'I don't know how I'm going to get any work done around here—he's so good-looking you wouldn't believe it. I almost fainted at his feet when I saw him. He must have thought I was mad.'

Katie laughed. 'I expect he was too busy finding his way around the place to notice.'

'He noticed you.'

'Did he?' Katie was surprised. 'When? How come I didn't see him?'

'You were talking to Craig and having a laugh. Neither of you was taking much notice of anything going on around you.'

'Oh, well…I expect he'll catch up with me later.' Katie turned her attention to her patient.

She was writing up her notes at the desk a little later when she saw Craig's patient walking towards the exit. He didn't look at all well, and he was squinting a little as though the light hurt him.

He appeared to stagger, and Katie was immediately concerned. She hurried over to him and helped him recover his balance. 'You don't look too good,' she said. 'Do you need to sit down for a while?'

'I think I'm going to be sick,' he muttered, and clutched his stomach. 'The pain in my head is driving me mad.'

Katie alerted Hannah, who hurried up with a bowl and a cloth. 'Have you seen the doctor?' Katie asked.

The man tried to nod and winced as though the effort was too much for him. 'He gave me a prescription.'

Katie glanced at the paper he held, and saw that it was a prescription for migraine medication. 'I think perhaps you had better lie down for a while,' she said. 'You don't look well enough to go anywhere just yet. I'll see if I can get hold of Dr Marshall and let him know what's happening.' She was surprised that Craig had sent him on his way in this condition, but perhaps the man's symptoms had worsened since then. She glanced at Hannah. 'Would you stay with Mr Framley? Cubicle two is empty. Perhaps he should go in there and lie down.'

Hannah nodded, and Katie turned to hurry away

and immediately found herself in collision with someone.

'Oh, I'm so sorry,' she began, struggling to right herself, her fingers meshing with a shirtfront and registering the hard wall of a man's chest. His heartbeat was strong and steady. She took a faltering step backwards and started to lift her gaze. 'I wasn't looking where I was going.'

'I guessed as much.' The deep voice had a familiar ring to it, and when she stared into the face of the man she gave a startled little jump.

'Drew? What are you doing here?'

'I work here. As of today, I'm your new consultant.' He looked at her assessingly. 'You seem to be in a bit of a hurry. Is that because of Dr Marshall's patient?'

She swallowed hard, trying to brace herself against the shock of seeing him here. 'I just thought I would alert him to the fact that the man wasn't very steady on his feet. There's no problem. We can deal with it. I imagine you must have plenty to be getting on with.'

Her mind was racing. She was worried that something wasn't quite right with the patient, but she didn't want to get Craig into any trouble. She was also finding it hard to take in what Drew had said. He was working here? How could that be?

She pulled in a deep breath and stared at him. 'Why didn't you tell me that you were going to be working here?'

'Has it come as such a shock to you?' he said. His

mouth was taut, and he must have seen how much it bothered her that he was here. 'I didn't tell you because I wasn't sure how things were going to work out,' he said, 'but as it happens they wanted me to start straight away. Mr Johnson, the consultant who was here before me, has had to take some compassionate leave. Family problems, they said, but they don't think he'll be coming back.'

Katie had heard that her former consultant was in a bit of a quandary. His son had been involved in an accident, and he had made up his mind to go and stay with him for a while. He had talked of finding work as a consultant near where his son lived. She said quietly, 'I heard that his son had multiple fractures, but as far as I know he's going to recover.'

'That's what I heard, too.' He glanced around. 'As for Dr Marshall's patient, I was just coming to take a look at him. I'm not satisfied that he's well enough to be discharged.'

Katie was distracted. From the set of his jaw she guessed that he was unhappy with Craig's diagnosis. She said flatly, 'Given the symptoms he presented with, I'm sure Dr Marshall thought he was doing the right thing. Headache and sickness are common symptoms of migraine.'

'Maybe.' Drew wasn't giving anything away. His mouth was set in a straight line and his eyes were dark as though he meant business. 'I'm going to take a look at him now. If you're not too busy, perhaps you would ask Dr Marshall to come and join me?'

Katie went and found Craig. She didn't like the fact that Drew had taken it on himself to intervene, but he was in charge now, and he was ultimately responsible for the actions of his colleagues.

'What's wrong?' Craig asked. He was in a cheerful mood, his hands in his pockets as he leaned against the desk in the middle of the room.

She explained the situation. 'I think your patient, Mick Framley, is unwell—at least, not well enough to go home just yet.'

'He was going to call for a taxi. I told him he needed to lie down in a darkened room.'

'I don't think he can make it home on his own.' She frowned. 'The new consultant, Drew Bradley, wants a word.'

'Does he?' Craig grimaced. 'I don't think he likes me very much. I've already had one run in with him today.'

'You have?' Her eyes widened. 'What was that about?' They were already walking back towards cubicle two.

'He seemed to be annoyed that I was talking to you. Apparently he thought my attitude was too casual and he wanted to know if I hadn't any work to be getting on with. He said I'd left a patient unsupervised.'

Katie frowned. 'I'm sorry. I didn't mean to get you into trouble.'

'It wasn't your fault. I think he was looking for someone to chew out.'

Was Craig right about that? Her own brother had said Drew could be ruthless, and she had tried to dismiss it, but now she was filled with doubt. It seemed unfair that Craig should fall foul of Drew this first day.

They had almost reached the cubicle by now, and Katie said, 'I'm a little worried about Mr Framley. He was complaining of neck stiffness, and he was hypertensive, too. Perhaps you should do a CT scan.'

'He didn't have any neck stiffness when I examined him,' Craig said defensively. 'There were no signs that led me to think of anything other than migraine.'

'It can be difficult to make an accurate diagnosis,' Katie said, 'but when you see the new consultant, be careful.'

'I will.' He pulled open the curtain of the cubicle and went in. Katie heard the murmur of voices, and guessed that he was talking to Drew. She hoped that he could put things right. She was beginning to suspect that Mr Framley was showing signs of a condition that was far more serious than Craig had guessed. In Craig's place, she would be doing a CT scan and blood tests, as well as an ECG and chest X-ray. From the looks of things, Mr Framley could be suffering from a subarachnoid haemorrhage.

A moment later, a worried-looking Craig came out from the cubicle. He looked white-faced, and Katie said anxiously, 'Can I help?'

He nodded. 'He's taken a sudden turn for the

worse, and we need to intubate. I'm going to call for a neurosurgeon.'

Katie went to assist, and the team went into action. Drew called for all the tests that she had guessed would be needed, and a short time later Mick went up to Theatre. Katie hoped that the surgeon would be able to save him. A bleed into the brain could kill a man unless it was caught in time.

Drew didn't comment on what had gone on between him and Craig, but he was tight-lipped whenever he was around him, and Craig was nervous for the rest of the day. Katie met up with him during a break in the afternoon, and he still looked anxious.

She put her hand on his arm. 'You should try not to worry too much,' she told him. 'You've only been in emergency medicine for six months. You can't get everything right all the time.'

His mouth made a bitter line. 'Try telling that to the new consultant. Mr Bradley doesn't seem to appreciate that he's here to support me. He thinks I missed the diagnosis because I didn't do the proper checks.'

'I'm sure you did what you thought was right at the time. I expect he'll get to know you better and see that he's being too hard on you.'

'Maybe. I just hope Mick Framley pulls through.' He moved his shoulders as though he was making an effort to shrug off his despondent mood and glanced at her thoughtfully. 'When I saw you talking to the

new man earlier, I had the feeling that you two knew
each other. Is that right? Is he from around here?'

'Yes, I do know him.' She pressed her lips together, uncertain how much she should say. 'He used
to live locally, but he moved away some years ago.
He was always determined to become a consultant in
A and E.'

'How was it that you got to know him?'

'We lived in the same neighbourhood at one time.
He was always around and about, and sometimes we
would find ourselves at the same functions.'

'Do you like him?'

Katie hesitated. It was a direct question, but she
could hardly tell Craig all the ins and outs of the
situation, all her doubts and insecurities, and in the
end she settled for an edited version of the truth.

'We used to get along all right. I've known him
since I was a teenager, and he went to the same school
as my brother, but I haven't heard from him these last
few years, and I think things are different now. He's
a consultant and he probably has a position to live up
to. You and I are just junior doctors, and we're worlds
apart from him, so we can't do anything other than
make the best of things.'

It seemed so long ago that Drew had been her
friend, her soul mate, someone who would step in and
intervene between her and her brother whenever they
had a falling-out. As a teenager Luke had been irre-
pressible in teasing and tormenting her, and even
when he'd got older, a student at university, he had

enjoyed provoking her. Drew had been someone she had been able to look up to and confide in, and now it seemed that all that had changed.

She went back to her patients and later on she attended to a man who had injured his hand at the factory where he worked. 'I'll put in a few stitches to hold the edges of the wound together,' she told him. 'Then I'll put a dressing over it and you'll need to come back to have the stitches removed in a few days. You should have an antibiotic, too, in case there's an infection.'

As she began to suture the wound, she saw Hannah pass by. 'Is there any news of Mr Framley?' she asked. 'He must be back from surgery by now.'

Hannah nodded. 'He's still in Recovery, but by all accounts things went reasonably well. The surgeon managed to deal with the aneurysm and patch him up.'

Drew came to watch as Katie put in the last suture. 'It'll be a while before the man is on his feet again,' he said, catching the end of the conversation. 'He was lucky that he hadn't left the hospital, and I guess that was down to you. By stopping him, you saved his life.'

'It was just fortunate that I happened to see him stagger.' She looked up at him, her green eyes troubled. 'It wasn't an easy diagnosis to make,' she said, wanting to defend Craig. 'Initially, he showed all the signs of having a migraine.'

Drew's gaze was flint sharp. 'We have to look beyond that. I hope your friend has taken the lesson on board.'

He had placed a slight emphasis on the word 'friend', and Katie glanced at him in dismay. His tone was cool, his jaw was set in a hard line, and she reflected that it was going to be difficult for Craig to make up for his lapse.

'I'm sure he'll take note, and learn from all the situations he comes across. I don't believe you can ask for any more.'

'Can't I?' His gaze shimmered over her. 'Then you don't know me very well, do you?'

He moved away from her, and Katie felt a small shiver go through her. Perhaps he was right. Perhaps she didn't know him at all.

CHAPTER THREE

'Is THIS for me? What is it? What did you buy me?' Four-year-old Reece clutched the parcel that Katie handed him, his eyes wide with excitement.

'Yes, it's for you. You'd better open it and find out,' Katie said with a smile. 'I hope you like it.'

Reece tore eagerly at the wrapping paper. 'Oh, wow,' he exclaimed. 'A train set. I love it, I love it.' He dashed off to show his mother, and Becky admired the toy and smiled.

'He's wanted one of those for ages,' she said.

Katie helped to undo all the packaging and hand out the various pieces, while Becky helped Reece to set up the train and track system. Reece's face was animated, his blue eyes shining, and Katie watched him with affection as he bent over the train set. His friends quickly gathered around him.

Luke came and stood by her side, and said quietly, 'I'm glad you were able to come today, Katie. I wasn't sure whether you would be working, but Reece wanted you to be here for his party.'

'I wanted to be here, too, so I arranged to swap shifts with Craig.' She smiled, glancing across the room. 'From the looks of things, Reece is having a wonderful time.' His fair hair was shining, illuminated by the sunshine that poured in through the living-room window.

Luke nodded. 'Becky wanted to make it special for him, and she worked hard to make sure that everything would be just right. She was on her feet all morning, preparing the food, while I was at work. I'm a bit worried that she's been doing too much, though. She doesn't look too well, does she?'

'I thought she was quite pale,' Katie said. Becky was fair-haired like her son, and she had a washed-out look about her today, as though something was not quite right. 'Is she still getting those same abdominal pains?'

'I think so. She doesn't tell me very much because she doesn't want to worry me. What do you think I should do?'

'I imagine the best thing would be for you to persuade her to have a word with her doctor or her obstetrician. If she's having any problems at all, I think she needs to get it checked out. Was everything all right at her last hospital appointment?'

'She said it was.'

'If I were in your shoes, I would get her to go and see the doctor in the next day or so, and perhaps you should go along with her. You can't be too careful. She's five months pregnant, isn't she?'

Before Luke could answer, Reece got to his feet and came over to them. 'Look, Daddy, look, Auntie Katie,' he said, waving his wooden train high in the air. 'Watch this. It goes over the bridge and through the tunnel.'

Katie went to take a look, squatting down to follow the train's progress as it raced along the track. Her brother followed. Parts of the track were raised up above the carpet, sloping, so that the wagons gathered speed as they went downhill. 'So it does,' Katie said approvingly. 'It's good, isn't it?'

'It goes well fast,' Reece said, looking pleased. He showed his friends, and even allowed one of the little boys to put another train on the track.

'You've quite a crowd here today,' Katie said to Becky.

Becky had been crouching on the carpet next to Reece, but now she got to her feet, wincing a little from the effort. 'We have. I'm glad so many of his friends were able to come today.'

'Do you want to go and sit down?' Katie asked, concerned that Becky was in some discomfort. 'You don't look too well, and I can take over for you, if you like. Just tell me what needs to be done and you can sit and supervise.'

Becky looked doubtful. 'Are you sure? I really feel as though I ought to be part of everything that's going on but I am feeling a bit under the weather today.'

'Of course I'm sure, and you'll still be in the middle of everything. Just tell me what you need me to do.'

'Thanks,' Becky said. 'I thought they could have a

game of Musical Chairs. At least I could work the music from my chair.'

'That's a good idea. I'll get the children organised and set everything up for you.'

Katie watched over the children for the next half-hour or so, and later, as she was serving out jelly and ice cream, Luke came to lend a hand and chatted with her.

'How are things going at work?' he asked. 'You said the other day that you were expecting a new consultant to take over. Has that happened yet?'

Katie nodded a little warily. 'He started the other day.'

'What's he like? Are you finding it easy to get along with him?'

She hesitated. 'I don't think you'll like what I'm going to tell you,' she said quietly.

Luke looked at her curiously. 'Why, what is it?'

'The new consultant is Drew Bradley.'

'Good heavens.' His face stiffened. 'You're joking, aren't you?' When he saw that she wasn't, he shook his head, frowning. 'That's hard to take in.' His mouth made a straight, hard line. 'Perhaps I should have guessed. I heard that his family is moving closer to the sea.'

It was Katie's turn to look surprised. 'I didn't know that.'

She was quiet for a moment, and Luke said, 'It must be difficult for you, working alongside him.'

'It's not quite as bad as I expected. He's given me

a fairly wide berth so far, but Craig isn't doing so well. Drew seems to be watching him every minute. I think he's afraid that he'll make a really bad mistake.'

'Is that likely?'

'I don't know. Craig is relatively inexperienced in emergency medicine, and he's not always as on the ball as he ought to be, but I think he'll find his feet in time. He's studying hard for his exams just now, and perhaps his concentration isn't what it should be. I think the fact that Drew is watching him so closely is making him nervous.'

'He needs to be careful. I heard that Drew caused a doctor to lose his job in the hospital where he worked up north.'

Katie frowned. 'How did you come to hear that? I didn't think you'd had any contact with Drew and his family these last few years.'

'His father has something to do with supplying local hospitals with equipment. That's probably one of the reasons why he's thinking of moving closer to where we are. In a way we're in competition with him, so I get to hear things from time to time. I don't know exactly what happened at Drew's previous hospital, but at any rate I think Craig should watch his step.'

The fact that Drew might have been involved in a doctor's dismissal was upsetting, and Katie wasn't at all sure what to make of it. She said slowly, 'I think you're probably right.'

She stayed with Luke and Becky for the rest of the evening; long after their young guests had gone home. Her parents were there, along with some friends of her brother and his wife, and they chatted over glasses of wine until it was quite late.

The next day, at work, Kate was still feeling the after-effects. 'Are you all right?' Craig asked. 'You look as though you could do with a coffee.'

She gave him a weak smile. 'That sounds wonderful, but I don't think there's time for that just yet. Hannah said that there's a patient coming in. Perhaps when things quieten down I'll get the chance.'

'How about a shoulder massage?' Craig said lightly. Gently, he began to knead the muscles of her neck and shoulders. 'That should make you feel a bit better. What was it, a late night?'

'Later than usual,' she admitted.

'I know all about those.' He gave a rueful chuckle. 'I've been trying to study, but it's hard to do that and to keep up a social life.'

Drew approached them and she stiffened a little, worried about what he might be thinking, seeing her with Craig this way. Craig let his hand drop from her shoulders, and Drew's gaze followed the movement, his eyes cool as he let his glance flicker over them both.

'I'd like a word with you, Dr Marshall, at the end of the shift,' he said flatly. 'We need to talk about your forthcoming review.'

Craig nodded, and Drew went on his way to look

at a set of X-rays. Craig winced. 'It looks as though I'm going to be in trouble again,' he said under his breath. 'I can't do a thing right, so what's the betting my review will be bad news?'

'It may not be as bad as you expect,' Katie murmured. Aware that Drew was casting them both a sidelong look, she started to walk away from the desk towards the ambulance bay.

'I wish I could be that confident,' Craig said walking by her side. 'Rumour has it that he had someone removed from his job at his last place. As far as I know, no patient was involved, so I don't know why it all got out of hand. I can't help wondering if I'm going to be next.'

'That could be just rumour, and nothing more,' Katie said. She remembered what her brother had said, but she was finding it hard to believe that Drew was capable of doing something like that without a good reason. Perhaps she was wrong about him, though.

Drew caught up with her later that morning. 'I thought you might be interested to know that our subarachnoid patient is still doing reasonably well. He's been admitted to the stroke unit, and they seem to think that he's young enough and has the stamina to pull through.'

'That's a relief,' she said. 'I was afraid that things might go badly for him. A lot of people die after a serious event like that.'

'He could have been one of those statistics, too, if

it hadn't been for your quick thinking. I dread to think what might have happened if he'd gone home.'

Katie glanced at him. 'It was thoughtful of you to check up on him—just as you checked up on the accident victims, the other day. Now you're a consultant, you must find that you're kept very busy, and that you have a lot of responsibility. It can't be easy to spare the time to follow up on everything.'

'That's true enough, but I went into the medical profession because I care about people, and for me the follow-up is part of what I'm about.'

Her expression was troubled. 'It shouldn't be just about the patients, though, should it? Being in charge means that you have to be responsible for colleagues, too, and sometimes they deserve a bit of leeway, don't you think?'

His mouth made a wry shape. 'Is this about Dr Marshall? You seem to be on very friendly terms with him, and you're very quick to jump to his defence. Do you think he needs to be protected?'

She said awkwardly, 'I just think that in your position a lot of the work is about supporting people, especially when it looks as though they're having some difficulties. Isn't that the mark of a good boss— that he's there to help his colleagues?'

'Of course it is. But the deal goes both ways. People who work here in emergency medicine have to be on top form, and give their best at all times. We can't afford to be casual about what we do.'

'I don't think Craig is casual.'

His eyes were intent as he studied her features. 'I hope he appreciates your concern for him. I'm not altogether sure that he deserves it.'

'But you've only been here for a short time. You don't know him very well.'

She might have said more, but a siren sounded in the distance and Katie looked over at Hannah, who was taking the call from the paramedics. The nurse briefly passed on the information, and Katie glanced at Drew and said, 'It sounds as though we've another patient coming in. I'd better get ready to receive her.'

'I'll come with you,' Drew said.

While they waited for the ambulance to arrive, Katie said conversationally, 'I heard that your family is moving closer to the coast. Is that true?'

'Yes, they're already there, in fact. I'm staying with them for the moment until I can find a place of my own.'

'Are you looking to rent?' she asked.

He shook his head. 'No, I want to buy a property.'

She sent him a sideways glance. 'You're not thinking of moving on, then?'

He shook his head. 'That wasn't part of my plan. This position is going to be made permanent, from what I've heard, because your former boss has made up his mind not to come back. His son is making a reasonable recovery, but he has a young family, and Tim and his wife decided that they wanted to be close by him for the long term.'

Katie was silent, absorbing that. When she looked

up, she saw that Drew was watching her, his eyes dark and brooding.

'Is that going to be a problem for you?' he said softly. 'Me being here, I mean.'

'No. Why should it be a problem? We work together, that's all, and I'm sure we can be professional about it.' She was worried, of course, because at the back of her mind she had wondered if this was just a temporary state of affairs, but now it seemed that she was going to have to rethink her position. How was she going to be able to work with him for the foreseeable future? She was on edge around him as it was.

The ambulance arrived, and as the paramedics wheeled their patient down the ramp, Katie hurried forward.

She stopped suddenly, shocked by what she saw. 'Becky?'

Drew was instantly alert. 'This is Becky, your sister-in-law?' He glanced at her quickly. 'Do you want me to take over?'

'No. I want to do this.' She was shaky, taken aback to see her brother's wife in a bad way. Even so, as they moved briskly towards the emergency room, Katie tried to comfort Becky. She was in obvious pain and was finding it difficult to talk, and Katie relied on hearing the paramedic's account of what was wrong.

'We were called out to attend to her at the roadside,' he said. 'She had managed to steer the car to

one side out of harm's way, and when we arrived she
was complaining of abdominal pains.'

'So she wasn't in an accident of any kind?'

'Not as far as we know.'

She listened to the rest of his report, and then
grasped Becky's hand. 'I'm going to take care of
you,' she assured her. 'Was Luke with you when you
were taken ill? Is he following?'

Becky shook her head. 'I was in the car on my
own,' she managed. 'He doesn't know anything about
what happened.'

'Don't worry. We'll get in touch with him.' Katie
signalled to Hannah, and as she quickly examined
Becky she outlined the situation to the nurse. Hannah
hurried away to try and get in touch with Luke, and
Katie continued with her examination. Reece would
be in nursery school at this time of day, so for the
moment at least they didn't have to worry about him.

Katie was very concerned about Becky's condition.
Her heart rate was too fast, the pain was radiating to
her back, pelvis and thigh, and she was feeling sick.

She was glad that Drew was working alongside her.
He was allowing her to take the lead, but it made her
feel more secure to have him there.

A few minutes later Katie moved away from the
bedside to consult with him. In an undertone, she said,
'I can feel a tender mass in her abdomen. I'm going
to do an ultrasound scan.'

Drew nodded. 'Ask Hannah to observe pulse and
blood pressure, and advise Theatre that we may have

a patient for them. It all depends what we find from the ultrasound.'

'She's pregnant,' Katie said anxiously. 'I'm worried about Becky *and* her unborn child.'

'I know. I'm concerned, too, but for the moment the baby seems to be coping. You'd better ask the obstetrician to come down here and take a look at her.' He gave her a searching look. 'There's another emergency coming in. Will you be all right here while I go and see to the new patient?'

Katie nodded. He was concerned enough to ask, and she wondered fleetingly why he didn't treat Craig with the same level of understanding.

She didn't dwell on it, though, but turned her attention back to her sister-in-law, speaking quietly to her, calming her.

There were beads of perspiration on Becky's brow, and Katie gently wiped them away.

'My baby,' Becky said tautly. 'You won't let anything happen to my baby, will you?'

'We're doing everything we can for both of you,' Katie reassured her. 'Just rest, and try not to worry.'

'But Reece is at nursery school. Who will fetch him when it's time for him to come home?'

There was panic in Becky's voice, and Katie said soothingly, 'It's all being taken care of. We're trying to get in touch with Luke, and I've asked Hannah to ring my mother and ask her to go and fetch Reece. All you have to do is lie back and let us do the rest.'

As soon as she was sure that Becky was composed,

Katie did an ultrasound scan, using a portable scanner. It took only a few minutes, but when she had finished she turned away to chat to the obstetrician and go and call for a surgeon.

Drew came over to her. 'What did you find?' he asked.

'She has what looks like an ovarian cyst,' she answered in a worried tone. 'It's caused an enlargement of the ovary and that in turn has made the ovary twist, so it's no surprise that she was in such a lot of pain.' Her brow furrowed in sympathy for her brother's wife. She said hurriedly, 'I've chatted with the obstetrician and we want to get her up to Theatre right away.'

Drew nodded. 'Concentrate on getting her up to surgery.' As she would have rushed away, he caught hold of her arm and steadied her. She looked at him, her green eyes full of anguish.

'I have to go,' she said, resisting.

He didn't release her. 'You need to try to stay calm,' he murmured. 'You've dealt with this kind of event before, and even though this is personal you must keep your composure and stay focussed. Can you do that?'

She nodded.

'All right. Take a few deep breaths before you go on.'

Katie wanted to resist and hurry away, but she did as she was told because she guessed that Drew would not let her go otherwise. Drawing air slowly into her lungs, she fought to regain her self-control.

The exercise did a lot to quieten her nerves, and she realised that Drew was right. She had been too anxious, too flustered, and that wasn't going to do any of them any good.

After a moment, feeling much more steady, she hurried away. She was glad that Drew had stopped her. Now she could think more clearly, and it was as though a fog had lifted from her mind and melted away.

When Luke arrived, he was in a bad state, and Katie drew him to one side.

'What's happening?' he asked. 'The police called me and told me that they had removed Becky's car because it was causing an obstruction. Has she been in an accident?' His face was pale and drawn. 'It's all my fault. We had words this morning. I was up-tight about the business and I wasn't really listening to what she had to say. In the end she went off in a huff. I should have been nicer to her.'

'No, it isn't your fault. She wasn't in an accident. She was in pain and she wasn't able to drive and someone called for the ambulance. We're taking care of her.'

'But where is she?' he asked, panicked. 'I want to see her.'

Drew came towards them. 'I'm sorry about what's happened to your wife,' he said. 'We're doing every-thing we can to help her. Do you and Katie want to go into my office to talk? You can be more private there.'

Luke ignored him, as though Drew had not spoken. Looking at Katie, he said, 'I want to see her.'

'That's not possible, at the moment,' Katie said. 'She—'

'I have to see her,' Luke cut in, his voice rising with agitation.

'She's gone up to Theatre,' Drew said quietly. 'She was suffering from a twisting of the ovary that was causing her a lot of pain. The surgeon will investigate the extent of the problem and then most likely he will remove the cyst and try to repair the torsion.'

'Is she going to be all right?' Luke turned to Katie, still paying no heed to Drew.

'I hope so. We'll know more in an hour or so.'

'And the baby?'

'They will do everything they can to make sure that Becky and the baby are safe. Try not to worry.'

Luke's mouth twisted. 'That's impossible.' His face seemed to crumple. 'I can't help thinking it was my fault. If she hadn't gone off in such a hurry—'

'No, you mustn't think that way,' Katie said. 'This was bound to happen. The pain she was getting over the last few days must have been the twisting starting in the ovary. There was nothing you could do to prevent that from happening. She's in good hands, Luke.'

Katie glanced at Drew. She was uncomfortable with Luke's dismissal of him, but there was nothing

she could do to put that right. Laying a hand on
Luke's shoulder, she said carefully, 'Shall we go into
Drew's office, as he suggested? I can make a cup of
coffee for you and we can talk. We won't know anything for a while yet.'

Luke nodded. 'I want to be around so I can go and
see Becky on the ward when she comes back from
surgery. What shall I do about Reece?'

'Mum said that she would collect him for you.'

'He can't stay at Mum and Dad's place for the
night, not with dad being the way he is at the moment.
Mum's got enough on her plate.' He looked at Katie
earnestly. 'Could you have Reece to stay with you,
just for tonight?'

'Of course.'

'Thanks.' He went with her into Drew's office and
she closed the door behind them, glancing worriedly
at Drew once more.

After a while she left Luke nervously sipping a cup
of coffee while she went to find out if there was any
more news.

Drew met her in the corridor and took her to one
side. 'How are you coping?' he asked. 'I know this
must be difficult for you.' He reached out and gripped
her arms in a comforting gesture. She felt the warmth
of his hands seeping through her thin cotton top, and
for a moment she wished that she could lean against
him and absorb some of his strength.

She didn't, though, and he looked into her eyes as
though he would read her thoughts. 'I'm all right,'

she managed. 'I just need to know that Becky has come through this, and that the baby has been unharmed.'

'We should have some news any time now.'

She sent him a quick look. 'I'm sorry for the way Luke treated you. He's not himself. He's worried about Becky.'

'You don't need to explain,' he said. 'I know how things are. I know that he still bears a grudge, but you don't have to concern yourself about that. I understand.'

'He feels resentful, because he has to help out with running the family business and it's not what he wanted originally. He wanted to concentrate on the design engineering side of things, and he was very good at that. I suppose he's battling with frustration all the time.'

'I know. I'm sorry that things turned out this way.' He studied her thoughtfully. 'At least you seem to be getting on better with your brother these days.'

She managed a weak smile. 'He used to tease me a lot, but he's grown out of that. It's true, we do get along much better.'

'I heard him ask you to take care of his little boy. Are you going to be able to manage that?'

'I think so. I hope so.' She glanced up at him. 'I should go back to work. I must find out if Becky is all right.'

Reluctantly, he let her go. She hurried away, anxious to discover whether Becky and her unborn baby had come through the surgery OK.

'I've managed to repair the torsion and I've dealt with the cyst,' the surgeon told her. 'She'll need to stay in hospital under observation for a few days because of the complication of her pregnancy. I don't think she's well enough to have any visitors just at the moment, but we'll look at the situation again in an hour or so.'

'Thank you.' She was thankful that the surgery was over at last, and she went back to relay the news to Luke.

'I'll stay here until she's well enough for me to see her, and then I'll see if I can make arrangements to stay here overnight,' he said. 'Are you going off duty soon?'

Katie nodded. 'I'll check on Becky before I go, and then I'll go and see Mum and Dad and pick up Reece. Try not to worry too much.'

'Thanks, Katie.'

When Katie left the hospital some time later, Becky was conscious but very weak, and they were monitoring the baby's condition as well as hers. 'We're concerned about the shock to her system,' a nurse told her. 'I'll let you know of any developments.'

Katie thanked her and went to pick up Reece. She had no idea how she was going to explain things to the little boy.

'Why my mummy not here?' he asked, frowning heavily.

'She's poorly,' Katie explained once again. 'She needs to rest for a few days in the hospital.'

'Me want go see her.'

Katie drew him into her arms and cuddled him. 'I know you do, sweetheart. As soon as she's well enough, I'll take you to see her.'

He was still troubled, and Katie said quietly, 'Tell you what—we'll make some play dough, and you can make a present for her. We'll bake it in the microwave, and then you can paint it. Would you like to do that?'

Reece nodded, and Katie breathed a sigh of relief. It wasn't much but it was a start.

Reece had a disturbed night. He woke up several times, wanting to know why his mother wasn't with him, and in the early hours of the morning, when Katie was asleep in her own bed, she woke to the sound of him crying. He was sleeping in the guest room, and she went in to him once more.

'I'm here,' she told him softly. She put her arms around him and gave him a hug. 'Were you having a bad dream?'

He nodded, rubbing the dampness from his eyes. She stroked his hair and did what she could to soothe his fears, holding him close until he was peaceful once more. He had been to Katie's house before, but he wasn't used to sleeping there overnight, and it was no surprise that he was feeling vulnerable. She sat by his bedside and tucked his teddy bear under the covers next to him as he closed his eyes.

'See Mummy 'morrow,' he mumbled.

'Yes,' she said. 'Soon.'

He was exhausted, but it comforted him to know that Katie was by his side, and eventually he dropped off to sleep once more.

After a few minutes, when she was sure that he was fast asleep, Katie slipped quietly out of the room and went downstairs. Her mouth was dry, and she could do with a drink of something cool.

The house was in semi-darkness, just a small lamp lighting the stairs. She went into the kitchen, and just as she was about to snap on the light in there she thought she heard a noise. It came from outside, in the garden, and it bothered her. It sounded as though someone or something was scurrying about out there.

She went to get a torch, and then quietly went out to see if she could discover what the disturbance was. In the darkness, though, everything was now silent. She flashed the torch around the garden, but there was no movement, except for the slight swaying of the branches of the trees caught by a faint breeze.

Frowning a little, she went back into the house. She felt shivery and a little afraid, and that wasn't how she was used to feeling. The house where she had once lived with her family overlooked the cottage, and she remembered that she had always felt safe there. It was empty now, though, and there wasn't even the comfort of knowing that she had neighbours to call on for help.

She was alone, and a little intimidated by the feeling of isolation. She locked the kitchen door, and then checked all the rooms just to make sure that everything was as it should be. Everything seemed to be in order, and she went back to bed and tried to get to sleep.

In the morning, she had to drag herself out of bed and rouse Reece to get him ready for nursery school.

'Shall we have some toast?' she asked him.

'With strawberry jam?' he said, eyes wide.

'If you like.'

Just a little while later, she was wiping sticky smears off his mouth and cheeks and they were laughing about the mess he had made.

She wasn't used to having any one else around first thing in the morning, but she muddled through, talking to him in as cheery a fashion as was possible, given how tired she was.

Just before she set off with him to go to nursery school, she made a quick check of the garden. A couple of fence panels were broken, and she stared at them, disturbed to see that the wooden slats were mangled and pushed to one side. There was no time to deal with it now, though. She had to get to work.

'You're looking very pale,' Drew said as she walked into A and E. He frowned. 'Are those shadows under your eyes? It looks as though you've had a bad night.'

'I've had better,' she told him. 'You don't need to be concerned, though,' she said defensively. 'I can still do my job well enough.' Was he going to watch her, the way he watched Craig?

'I'm sure you will. What was the trouble—problems with the little boy?'

She nodded. 'He was missing his mum.'

'Has there been any news?'

'She's still in quite a lot of pain.' She grimaced. 'I popped in to see her this morning first thing, and they were worried about her blood pressure. Thankfully, the baby seems to be doing all right.'

'That's something at least.'

'I know, but I can't help worrying about Becky. She seems very frail.'

Drew put his arm around her shoulders. 'It's a bad time for you. If there is anything I can do to help, you only have to ask.'

She looked up at him, warmed by his touch, tempted by his nearness, but at that moment she saw that her brother had come through the swing doors and was walking towards her. She was alarmed in case he had witnessed their brief embrace. She couldn't help herself, but her instant reaction was to stiffen and draw back from Drew.

He must have known why she had done that. He let his arm fall away from her and then he turned and walked away towards the desk. He picked up a patient's chart and headed for a cubicle. His jaw was hard, his mouth set in a straight line. He was annoyed by her reaction.

Her brother hadn't noticed anything amiss, but

Katie was still tense. It was hard, working with Drew, getting to know him all over again and feeling the tug of her emotions pull her in all directions. How could she allow herself to lean on him and accept his support when her family was so antagonistict towards him?

CHAPTER FOUR

'I'M GLAD I found you still on duty.' Katie's father smiled at her. 'We haven't seen so much of you lately since you've been looking after Reece.'

It had been a few days since Becky had been taken ill, and Reece was still staying at Katie's house while Luke sorted himself out. Her father looked a little anxious. 'Is it all right if I stop and talk to you for a minute or two? I know how busy you are.'

'Of course. I was just about take a short break and get some coffee,' Katie answered. She glanced at him. His face was pale and he was a little out of breath. She could hear the wheeze of his chest. 'I wasn't expecting to see you until later on today. Is everything all right?'

'Things are fine. I came into the hospital for my appointment with the specialist, and I thought I'd come and see you on the off chance that you could spare a few minutes.'

'We can go along to the doctors' lounge. It's this way.'

She walked along the corridor with him, but as they were about to turn into the doctors' lounge Katie saw that someone was heading in their direction. He was glancing around him and he appeared to be in a great hurry, so she quickly stepped aside out of his path.

The man must have realised that he had almost run into her because he stopped and looked around. 'Sorry, I was heading for the manager's office. Too busy looking for signs to notice where I was going.' He made a half-smile and then halted, looking at them in sudden recognition. 'David... Katie... I had no idea that you were here.' Jacob Bradley stared at them.

Katie said slowly, 'I think that works both ways.' Her father had frozen by her side, as though seeing his old enemy had pinned him to the spot.

Jacob glanced awkwardly back and said to her father, 'Drew told me that you were ill. I'm sorry to hear that.'

Katie glanced at her father. He made to no attempt to reply, and his features had hardened into a rigid mask.

Jacob said a little stiffly, 'I wonder if we might find an opportunity to get together when my meeting here has finished? It's such a long time since we saw each other last.'

'I think we said all we needed to say some years ago.' Her father started to turn away.

Katie looked from one to the other worriedly. She felt that there ought be something she could do to bridge the gap between them, but while she was seeking the words Drew came along and intervened.

'Dad, I've been looking for you.' He must have

taken in the situation at a glance because he added briskly, 'Perhaps I should take you along to Administration. Your appointment's in just a little while, isn't it?'

'That's right.' Jacob hesitated, looking back at Katie's father. He didn't say any more, though, and perhaps it was just as well because her father's mood was grim.

Katie sent Drew a worried look. Any hope of reconciliation seemed to have flown out of the window, and she was left with a sense of emptiness. Until now she hadn't realised how much she had hoped that things could be squared and the past forgotten. Drew had been part of her life for such a long time, until everything had gone wrong. She still cared about him, and deep down she had always held onto the dream that things might go back to how they had been before, but she saw now that that was an empty dream. Nothing was going to change.

Drew led his father away, and Katie opened the door of the doctors' lounge. She ushered her father into the room, and then went to pour coffee for them both.

'I'm sorry about that,' she murmured. 'I had no idea that he was in the hospital.'

'Let's forget about it, shall we?'

She nodded, and handed him a cup. 'What did the specialist have to say?'

'He wants to put me on some new medication to thin my blood. Then they want to do some kind of treatment to steady my heartbeat. He says it's far too erratic.' He frowned. 'Anyway, he can't do it yet, he says. He needs to make sure there are no blood clots that are going to cause any damage.'

'Are you happy about that?'

'I think so, but I can't say that I really understand what this cardiac conversion is.'

'It means that he'll shock the heart to try to get it back to a steady rhythm. You shouldn't feel anything, because he'll give you an anaesthetic when he does it. He can't do the procedure, though, while there is any risk of clots forming, and that's why he needs to thin your blood first. He will probably keep you on the medication for a while and then check how things are going. After that, he'll be able to give you a date to come into hospital.'

'As long as he can get me back on my feet. That's all I'm worried about really. I need to get back to work.'

Katie shook her head. 'I don't think you're well enough just yet.' She went and sat with him by the table at the side of the room. 'You've had quite a few setbacks and these last few months have been difficult for you. I think you should forget about work for the time being.'

'That's easier said than done. I have to do something. Now that Luke is spending a lot of his time at the hospital with Becky, there's no one to take care of the business.'

'I thought he was keeping in touch with things

from here. He said he was making calls and organ-
ising things.'

'It's true, he is, but we've had some queries for
new orders, and we can't afford to let them go. I need
to be in the office myself so that I can oversee things.'

Katie frowned. 'Perhaps I could do something to
help?'

He shook his head. 'I know you mean well, but we
need somebody experienced. The secretary can deal
with all the day-by-day stuff, but the rest of it needs
to be handled by someone with specialist knowledge.'
He made a face. 'We're dealing with sensitive equipment, monitors for neonatal units. We can do so much
good if only we could persuade the hospital management to consider buying from us. It just makes me so
mad that Jacob Bradley sails through life with hardly
any effort, and yet he manages to get contracts locally.'

'He's not developing quite the same kind of equipment as you, though, is he? The monitors that he's
providing have a more widespread use, don't they?
It's probably because your equipment is so speciali-
sed that you're finding trouble marketing it. With hospital budgets being what they are, management probably don't like to take risks with anything new. They
perhaps need an effective demonstration of how the
equipment works.'

'You might have a point there,' her father mused.
He looked thoughtful. 'I've always placed the emphasis on what we can provide, rather than comparing

it to what's in common use at the moment, and how our equipment is different. Perhaps it's the marketing that we need to concentrate on—showing the administrators what they stand to gain by trying out our product. Perhaps I can work something out where they get to work with it for a while before they buy.'

He looked a bit brighter now, and Katie was relieved about that. It seemed to her that life could be very unfair. Things had always come easily to Drew's father. He had never had to struggle for anything, and it was upsetting that her father was having such a hard time of it.

'I really think you need to get someone else in to help out,' she said. 'I know that can be expensive, but perhaps you could call on an agency for help? That way, you're only employing someone's expertise on a temporary basis.'

'That's worth thinking about.' He nodded. 'With my health not being so good these days, I've fallen into a bit of a rut. I'll have to think a little differently and see what I can come up with.' His mouth made a wry shape. 'I can't let Jacob Bradley have it all his own way.'

They talked for a while longer, and then Hannah put her head around the door, and said, 'We've an emergency coming in. Ten minutes, tops.'

'I'll be right with you.' Katie got to her feet. 'I'm sorry, Dad, but I have to get back to work.'

He smiled. 'It's all right. I know how things are.' He went with her to the door.

She saw him out to the car park, and then went back to the emergency room to ready herself for the next patient.

Drew was there, dealing with a patient who had a head injury. He gave her a quick look. 'I gather your father was here for an appointment. I thought he looked more tired than usual.'

'He's tired of battling with the competition. Your father, in particular.' She didn't bother to hide her pent-up feelings. 'He seems to have been at the root of all my family's troubles.'

'Perhaps it's time that you and your family started to try to make the best of things as they are. You're not going to achieve anything by dwelling on what happened years ago.'

Katie didn't answer. He was probably right, but that didn't help to make her feel any better about the situation. Resentment was still bubbling away inside her.

The paramedics brought in a middle-aged man who was suffering from severe abdominal pain, and Katie went forward to receive him.

'He collapsed in the street,' the paramedic told her. 'Somebody called the ambulance, but no one seemed to know what happened, except that he'd suddenly crumpled. He recovered a little on the way here, but he hasn't been able to tell us very much.'

'Thank you. I'll take it from here.' She turned to her patient. 'We're going to take good care of you, Mr Mitchell,' Katie said quietly, trying to reassure him. 'I understand that this pain came on very suddenly, is that right?'

The man nodded. He could barely get his words out, and Katie could see that there were beads of sweat on his brow. 'It seems to be spreading everywhere,' he muttered. 'My groin, my hips.'

Katie checked his blood pressure. It was very low, and his heart rate was very fast. He was pale, and when she examined him, she was worried. Turning to Hannah, who was assisting, she said, 'I'm going to do an ultrasound scan. He'll need chest and abdominal X-rays. We better get any ECG reading, too.'

She turned back to James Mitchell. 'I want you to keep the oxygen mask over your face,' she told him. 'It will help you to breathe more easily. I'll give you something for the pain, and something to stop you from being sick. Then I'm going to try to get some more fluids into you.' She was concerned about his condition, worried that he might be descending into shock, and she worked quickly, obtaining IV access and sending blood to the lab for tests.

'Is there anyone we can contact for you?' she asked when it looked as though he was feeling a little more comfortable.

He shook his head. 'There's no one.'

Katie frowned. 'No wife or family?'

'No one.' His voice sounded harsh, rough around the edges, and it might have been the effort of speaking, but Katie couldn't be sure about that.

'What about brothers or sisters?' It was hard to

believe that there was no one in the world who cared about this man.

'I had a brother.' His teeth were gritted. 'We haven't seen each other in years.' He made a face, and there was an empty look in his eyes. 'We had an argument.'

It was so sad to think that there was no one to come and comfort him. 'I'm sorry.' She touched his shoulder lightly in a gesture of reassurance. 'Try to get some rest. I'll go and take a look at your test results and see if I can find out what's happening.'

'You look worried,' Drew said as she went over to the desk. 'Is there a problem?'

'Nothing that I can't handle,' she said. 'At least, not so far.'

'What do you think is wrong with your patient?'

'I suspect that he has an aortic aneurysm. I'm afraid that it might have already ruptured, and that he's haemorrhaging inside. He's going into shock.'

'What are you doing about it?'

'I'm going to call for a vascular surgeon and an anaesthetist to come down here and look at him.'

Drew frowned. 'If he's already going into shock, that could tip him over the edge.'

She nodded. 'I know. I'm doing what I can for him. I'm just worried that it won't be enough.'

'Does he have any relatives? They need to be here.'

'I think there's a brother.' She grimaced. 'They had a falling-out some years ago apparently, and he appears to be wary of getting in touch.' She sent Drew an anxious look. 'I think I ought to try to find him and contact him, don't you?'

'It would probably be as well. If anything happens, this is probably going to be the last chance they will have to be reunited.'

'I'll get onto the patients welfare department. Perhaps they'll be able to come up with something.'

First, though, she arranged for the surgeon and the anaesthetist to come down, and then she went back to her patient. She didn't know if it would be possible to find James Mitchell's brother, but she would do her best. It was such a sad situation to be in, having no contact with your family, and she could imagine that the loneliness would be unbearable.

In a way it reminded her of what had happened in her family. At least they were united, but the argument and the falling-out with Drew's family had brought about consequences that had gone on for years and seemed insoluble.

She did what she could for James Mitchell, but when her shift came to an end he was still in a critical condition and, despite several phone calls, she had made no headway in finding his brother. James had been sent up to Theatre, and the surgeon had done what he could to stem the bleeding and repair the aneurysm, but it was touch and go whether he would survive.

She went and collected Reece from her parents' house. 'We'll go and get some tea, shall we?' she said, taking him into the kitchen. 'What would you like? Dippy egg and soldiers?'

Reece nodded, but his mind was somewhere else. 'Why my daddy not come home?' he asked.

'He's staying with your mummy at the hospital,' she explained. 'Your mummy's still poorly, and she needs to stay in bed for a while.' He was frowning, and she said quietly, 'You've seen your daddy today, though, haven't you? He took you to nursery school, didn't he?'

Reece nodded. 'Me wanted see my mummy, but Daddy said no. Not yet, he said.' He thrust out his mouth in a belligerent expression. 'Me want see my mummy. Why my daddy not take me?'

'I'm sure he will take you to see her,' she said. 'Perhaps he thinks Mummy needs to rest for a little while until she's stronger.' She wondered if she needed to speak to Luke. Perhaps he didn't realise how important it was for his son to go and see her. She guessed that Becky would want see Reece, too, but perhaps Luke was being over-protective. 'I'll talk to your daddy about it.'

She put bread on the grill pan, and added, 'I bought you some scissors and glue and some coloured paper. I thought you might like to make Mummy a picture. Would you like to do that?'

'Some flowers?' he said. 'Mummy would like flowers.'

'That's a really good idea,' she said. 'You have a

think about what you want to do while I get the tea ready, and then we'll sit down and do it together.'

Reece went and fetched his sketchbook and began to draw. He looked a little more cheerful now, and Katie watched him with affection. He was a lovely boy, and Becky and Luke could be proud of him. It was so upsetting that Becky was still in hospital. The operation had taken a lot out of her, and they were still worried about her raised blood pressure. They were doing all they could to protect her and her unborn baby.

As she had promised, she sat with Reece after tea and together they made a picture, sticking oddly shaped flowers and leaves that curled and drooped onto a sheet of paper. They finished it off with a strange-looking basket that Reece had cut and coloured.

'Your mummy will love that,' Katie told him, and he gave her a beaming smile, full of satisfaction.

Later, when she settled him down for the night in bed, she kissed his soft cheek and stroked his hair. 'Goodnight. little one. Sweet dreams.'

He was tired, and he fell asleep quickly. Katie went downstairs and did a few chores, before settling down in the armchair with a book to read.

She couldn't concentrate. The words were meaningless to her. Her mind kept turning back to Drew. Every day she worked with him, alongside him, and every day she wished that things could go back to the

way they had been before, when they had been
friends…when they had been more than friends.

It wasn't going to happen. There was still a huge
gulf between them.

Restlessly, she put the book to one side. It was
growing dark now, and she went over to the window
to draw the curtains. The garden was shadowed, and
she could no longer make out the colours of the flowers or the shrubs, but there was movement out there,
something stirring among the trees. She couldn't
make out what it was.

She still hadn't had time to repair the fence, and
now it bothered her that someone or something might
be gaining access to the garden. Conscious of Reece
asleep in bed, she knew that she had to make sure
that all was well.

She went and fetched the torch from the cupboard
and quietly went outside. Now she could hear strange
sounds in the garden, as though someone was creep-
ing about. She flashed the torch so that its beam lit
up the bushes.

'Who's there?' she called out sharply. 'Whoever
you are, you'd better show yourself.'

There was an odd, scuffling noise and then a man's
figure came out of the darkness. She stood very still,
stiffening.

'You can just stop right there,' she said in a tight
voice. Inside, she was shaking, frightened out of her
wits. What if he was strong enough to overpower her?

'I don't know what you're doing here, but this is private property.'

'I didn't realise that anyone would be about at this time of night.' The voice was muffled, and there was another odd sound, like the rustle of leaves, as though he was poking around in the bushes. Katie's imagination started to work overtime. She conjured up the vision of someone in a Balaclava, brandishing a stick. 'Just don't come any closer,' she said on a warning note. 'How did you get in here? Are you responsible for breaking the fence?'

'The fence was broken already,' he said. 'That was nothing to do with me.'

There was another rustling sound and then a black shape made its way towards her. She backed away at the sound of heavy breathing.

'Don't come any nearer.' She was waving a torch around, but the man seemed to have disappeared, melting into the background of the bushes.

'I didn't mean to frighten you.' The voice was close now, and she realised that the man had come up alongside her.

'Keep away. I have an iron bar here and I'm not afraid to use it,' she lied in panic.

'Please, don't do that. I bruise easily.'

A waft of hot air fanned against her leg, and then something brushed her skirt. She jumped back in alarm and stumbled over the uneven ground.

A pair of strong arms caught her, encircling her, and she found herself drawn close to a man's hard chest. She lost her grip on the torch, and it fell to the ground with a thud.

'Katie, it's all right… It's me— Drew. I didn't realise that this was your garden. I really didn't mean to make you afraid.'

'Drew?' She wished that she could see his face. 'Is it really you? What are you doing here?'

'I was just looking for my dog. We were taking a walk along the lane when he ran off. He must have come through the hole in the fence.'

'I didn't know that you had a dog.' His arms were warm and strong around her, and she welcomed their refuge. She was still shaking a little.

'Do you really have an iron bar?'

'No. It just made me feel safer to say that.'

He chuckled, a soft rumbling sound that started in his throat. 'Thank heaven for that. You had me worried for a minute.' He glanced around. 'I don't know what's happened to Bugsy. He's probably poking around in the bushes somewhere. Shall we go into the house? I think perhaps you need to sit down and recover from the shock.'

'I think you're right. Will the dog come if you call him?'

'He usually does, providing that he's not sniffing something particularly interesting. Is it all right with you if he comes into the house?'

'Yes. Bring him into the kitchen.'

He called the dog's name, and Bugsy came towards them in a rush. As they drew closer to the kitchen,

and the light, she could see that he was a border col-
lie, black and white, obviously not very old.

'How do you manage to look after a dog?' she
asked. 'You're out at work a lot of the time.'

'My parents look after him some of the time, or
my brother and his wife watch out for him. I bought
him as a guard dog...' He broke off, smiling, and
then added, 'And I gave him a name to go along with
that...like the gangsters, you know...but I don't think
he's going to be too good at his job.' He grinned.
'I've always wanted a dog, and as soon as I bought
the house I knew I would have room for him to roam
about comfortably.'

Drew was still holding her as he led her into the
kitchen. She was glad of that. She was afraid that if
he let her go her legs would crumple beneath her.

'How long have you had the dog?' she asked when
they were safely in the kitchen. They left the door
open while they waited for the dog. He seemed to
have gone exploring once more.

'A few months. He's still a pup, though from the
size of him you wouldn't know it. He's not used to
his new surroundings yet, otherwise I don't think he
would have come in to your garden. I'm still trying
to train him.'

He looked down at her. 'Are you feeling a little
better now? Your heart was racing so fast, I thought
you might collapse on me.'

'I'm OK. This is the second time I've heard an

intruder in the garden. I didn't know what I was up against.'

He nodded. 'I've seen some youths hanging about. They didn't look as though they were up to much good, and they are probably responsible for the broken fence. I'll have a word with them next time I see them.'

'Thanks. I'll have to get it fixed.'

'I can see to that for you. I'll bring my tools over tomorrow, if you like.'

Katie looked up at him. It was hard to believe she was having this conversation. He had come out of nowhere, and now he was in her kitchen, and she was locked in his embrace. It seemed so right, a perfect place to be.

The kitchen door opened, and a sleepy little voice said, 'Why you holding my auntie? Who are you?'

They both turned around. Reece was a tiny figure in the doorway, and Katie came to her senses and broke away from Drew. She went over to Reece and lifted him up in her arms.

'What are you doing out of bed, little man?'

'Me want drink.' He squinted at Drew, and said huskily, 'Who are you? What you doing here?'

Drew smiled at him. 'I work with your auntie at the hospital. You must be Reece. I've heard about you.'

'Are you looking after my mummy? My mummy's poorly. She got a baby in her tummy.'

'I know she's poorly. Some other doctors are looking after your mummy.'

Katie settled Reece down on a chair by the kitchen table. 'I'll get you some milk,' she said softly.

Drew came and sat down at the table with Reece. 'Are you pleased that your mummy's having a baby? Do you want a little brother or a little sister?'

Reece shrugged. 'Me wanted a set of soldiers with fire guns, but Mummy said not till Christmas.' He looked peeved. 'That's long time away.'

The puppy came in through the kitchen door and Drew went to greet him, stroking his head. Then he shut the door to prevent him from wandering off again.

'It's a doggy,' Reece exclaimed gleefully. 'What's his name?'

'Bugsy.'

'Bugsy.' He laughed. 'Is he your doggy?'

'That's right, he is,' Drew said. 'He's not very good at doing what he's told just yet, but I'm working on that.'

Reece jumped down from his chair and went over to the dog. Bugsy's tail wagged joyfully, and the two of them began to race around the kitchen. It was difficult to know who was chasing whom.

Katie said quietly to Drew, 'If you're walking your dog around here, then you must be living close by. I didn't know that you'd managed to find a house.'

'I did. I've just moved in, but I'm still living out

of crates at the moment.' He sent her a guarded look, and she wondered what was on his mind.

'You didn't mention it at work. You must have moved pretty quickly to find a place. There aren't that many up for sale round here.'

'That's true. When this one came up for sale, I acted straight away. I offered the full asking price and it was taken off the market the same day that it went on sale.' He was still looking at her with a faintly odd expression, and she suddenly felt a frisson of doubt run through her.

'Where is this house?' she said.

'Just across the way. It more or less backs onto this one.'

She stared at him, a chill making its presence felt along her spine. 'You've bought my house, haven't you?'

He shook his head. 'Not exactly. It's not really your house. At least it hasn't been your house for some time.'

Her mouth straightened. 'Don't play games with me, Drew. You know full well what I mean. You've bought my family home, haven't you?'

He nodded. 'It's a beautiful old house. I always liked it. When it came on the market, I knew that it was the house I wanted. I didn't mean to hurt you. I know how much the place meant to you and your family.'

'I can't believe that you would do this to me, to my family. How did you expect me to feel?'

He shrugged lightly. 'I suppose I hoped you would understand. We all have to move on and, from what I heard, your parents wouldn't be able to buy it back again. I'll take care of it, Katie, I promise.'

She shook her head. Pain ran through her chest. It was hard to take in what he had done. How could he do something so hurtful? She had thought she'd known him, but she didn't really know him at all, did she?

CHAPTER FIVE

'WE'VE just been to see Becky,' Katie's mother said. 'She's looking much better, but they still want to keep her in hospital and under observation for a while longer.'

'It's been a worrying time,' Katie answered, 'for all of us.' They were sitting in the hospital café, chatting over a cup of coffee while Katie took her mid-morning break. The café overlooked a quadrangle, decorated with stone tubs that overflowed with bright flowers.

'Are you coping all right with Reece?' Her mother's grey eyes were troubled. 'I know that Luke is finding all of this very difficult, and he worries that he's putting too much on your shoulders. He's dividing his time between work and the hospital, and I know he looks forward to being with Reece when he comes out of school. It's just the evenings that are difficult. He wants to spend as much time as possible with Becky, and it makes it easier for him if Reece stays with you overnight. He doesn't have to rush away from the hospital for Reece's bedtime, and he doesn't have the worry of getting him ready for school in the morning.'

'So far, everything has worked out all right. I like

having Reece with me. He's a dear little boy, and he's hardly any trouble. I've just had to be more organised than usual, that's all. To be honest, I don't think Luke would manage the breakfast routine without Becky to oversee things. He was never at his best first thing in the morning.'

'I wish your dad and I could help out more.'

Katie shook her head. 'I know that it's awkward for you just now, and having a little boy running about the place and causing mayhem wouldn't be a good idea. You'd be on edge all the time, because you never know if Dad is going to suffer a relapse, do you? How is he managing with the new medication?'

Her mother frowned. 'I'm not sure. He seems to be bruising very easily.'

'Perhaps you need to go back to the doctor and get the dosage adjusted.'

'Yes. I'll try to persuade him.' She made a wry smile. 'You know how difficult your dad can be. He hates to think that he's being a nuisance, and I keep telling him it's his health that's at stake.'

'Has he sorted out his problems with the business? I know that he was worried now that Luke is spending such a lot of his time with Becky.'

Her mother grimaced. 'He's making some headway. He contacted an agency, as you suggested, and he's trying to win some new orders. It's not easy for him, and he gets so riled when he sees that Jacob

Bradley has managed to obtain a another contract—here in this hospital. Can you believe it?'

'I heard something about that,' Katie admitted. 'As far as I know, we're getting some new equipment for the laboratory—something to make the test procedures more accurate.'

'I expect your boss had something to do with that.' She said it with a curl of her lip. 'I don't know how you can work with Drew after what his family did to us. It must be really hard for you to see him here, day after day.'

Katie frowned, at war with herself. There was always going to be this nagging conflict between her feelings for Drew and her loyalty to her family. 'It wasn't as though I planned it.'

Her mother touched her arm. 'I'm sorry. I shouldn't have said that. I wasn't blaming you. You mustn't think that. It's just that things seem so unfair sometimes, especially when I see Jacob Bradley having it all his own way. He must have had some help from Drew. It's too much of a coincidence otherwise.'

'Not necessarily. I'm not sure how much influence Drew would have when it comes to management decisions. Mostly the buying of equipment is left to the administrators.'

'I imagine he must have had a word in their ears.' Her mother glanced at her watch. 'I must go and find your dad. Last time I saw him, he was buying some flowers for Becky from the hospital shop. We'll drop them off and make our way home.'

'Give Becky my love. Tell her I'll pop in and see her on my lunch-break, will you?'

'I'll do that. I'll see you later, Katie. I know you have work to get on with.'

Katie watched her mother go off in the direction of the hospital shop, and then she made her way back to A and E. It was a thorny situation to be in, knowing that her mother was hostile towards Drew. It made her position here even more awkward.

Craig was standing by the desk, signing off some charts, and she went to join him. She wanted to look for details of her next patient, and at the same time she wanted to check whether there had been any progress in finding James Mitchell's brother. James had struck a chord with her, and she had made enquiries about him earlier that day. The ward sister reported that he was still in a very bad way, and that it was touch and go whether he would survive. Katie was anxious to sort something out before the worst happened.

'How are things?' she asked. Craig was pale, she thought, and bleary-eyed. 'We were rushed off our feet first thing, weren't we? You didn't look as though you were coping too well. Is it still as hectic here?'

'It's not too bad, I suppose.' He made a face. 'I think I've got a cold coming and it's making my head muzzy. The patients keep giving me odd looks, as though they're afraid I'm going to cough all over them.'

'Oh, dear. I expect they have enough to worry

about without that. Perhaps you should get an early night. See if you can chase the cobwebs away.'

'That's a good idea,' he said with a grin. 'How do you feel about joining me? I'll take a couple of aspirin and get myself on top form.'

She shook her head. 'You never give up, do you?' she said with a smile.

She was suddenly aware that they were not alone. Craig straightened up and his face took on a guarded look as a shadow fell across them.

She glanced sideways and saw that Drew had come up alongside them. Guiltily, she wondered how much of their conversation he had heard, but then she took herself in hand. Why was she being so defensive? Her private life was her own, and why should she care what he thought? He hadn't given her feelings any heed when he had bought her family home, had he? She braced her shoulders.

'I'd like a word with you, Craig,' Drew said. There was a taut edge to his mouth and Katie wondered what Craig had done wrong now. 'My office, I think.'

'I was just going to see another patient,' Craig murmured. 'Can it wait till later?'

'No, I'm afraid it can't.' Drew's expression was uncompromising. 'I'm sure that Katie won't mind taking over from you for a few minutes.' He turned to Katie. 'Is that all right with you?'

She nodded. She was about to pick a chart from the tray when Drew stopped her. 'There's a patient in cubicle four. Perhaps you would take a look at him for me.'

'All right.' Before she did that, she asked the desk clerk to contact the patients' welfare office once more to see whether James Mitchell's brother might have some connection with the local boating industry. James had told her that they used to be fishermen together, but they had given up the trade and gone their separate ways. James had turned his back on the sea, but that wasn't necessarily true of his brother.

A few minutes later, she went to do as Drew had asked. The patient was a child, she discovered, a young boy of around six years old. His mother was sitting with him, and she looked anxious, her whole manner restless and on edge. The child was pale and thin.

'Hello, Sam. Hello, Mrs Slater.' Katie smiled at the woman and the boy, and then she sat down beside them and glanced at her notes. A small line indented her brow. 'I understand that you asked for a second opinion. Would you like to tell me what the problem is?' It was unusual for a parent to request such a thing in A and E, but it wasn't unheard of.

'I brought Sam here because he was complaining of chest pain. He's been very tired lately and a little breathless sometimes. One day last week he fainted, and it happened again today. I couldn't get hold of my own doctor, so I brought him here.'

Katie glanced at her notes again. 'You saw another doctor here earlier today?'

'Yes, that's right. He talked to us for a while, but he didn't seem to take on board what I was saying. I told him that I thought there was something not quite right…'

She glanced at her son and pulled in a quick breath, and Katie guessed that she didn't want to say anything to alarm the boy. 'I told him that I thought we needed some tests done so that we could find out what the problem was, but he said that he thought Sam was worried about starting school at the end of the summer.' She made a face. 'He's going into a new class. A couple of his friends have moved away from the area and he's a little anxious about that, but I don't think that's what's causing his problem.'

Katie studied Craig's sprawling handwriting. 'I believe the doctor you saw suggested that Sam might also have a chest infection. He was going to prescribe an antibiotic.'

Mrs Slater said calmly, 'I'm sure that he did what he thought was right, but I would feel happier if you would look at Sam again. I'm his mother, and I don't believe this is down to nerves or a simple infection. I'm not saying he doesn't have an infection, but these incidents have been going on for some time now, and I want to know what's causing them. There's something wrong with him, and I want to know what it is. I asked your consultant if he would allow someone else to look him over.' She grimaced. 'No disrespect to you, but I was hoping he would do it himself. Unfortunately, he said that he was busy just then with another patient, and that he had to be somewhere else very shortly and couldn't follow it through.'

Katie nodded and thumbed through the notes once more. 'As I understand it, your GP has seen Sam about his condition. Is that right?'

'Yes, he has, but he put it down to nerves, too.' Mrs Slater's features became taut. 'I don't believe that's the answer. I think my GP thought I was just being over-protective, but I'm not. I'm concerned, and I'm tired of being fobbed off.'

Katie gave her a gentle smile. 'All right. Let's see if we can get to the bottom of this, shall we? I'll start by examining Sam again.' She turned to the boy. 'I'm going to ask you to lift your T-shirt again, Sam, so that I can listen to your chest with my stethoscope. Are you OK with that?'

Sam nodded, looking at her with a wide-eyed expression, and Katie carefully examined him. After a moment, she said, 'Do you want to listen to what I'm hearing? There are lots of funny squishy sounds going on in there.'

He nodded and she placed the earpieces in his ears. Awestruck, he listened.

'OK, Sam,' she said after a little while. 'I'll put my stethoscope away now, and you can pull your T-shirt back down.' She wound the instrument up and put it in the pocket of her white coat. 'Tell me about the fainting,' she said. 'When did it happen? What were you doing just before you fainted?'

'I was playing hide and seek,' Sam said. 'We were

in my friend's garden, and I went up the steps to see if I could hide among the bushes. Everyone else was hiding around the side of the house or next to the shed, and I didn't think Jason would find me there.' He pulled a face. 'I started to feel a bit funny, and then I sort of fell down, and Jason went and fetched his mother.'

'Thanks, Sam. You did very well.'

His mother said, 'Do you know what's the matter with him?'

Katie turned to look at Mrs Slater. 'Not just yet. I'm going to do a few tests.'

'What sort of tests?'

Katie glanced at Sam who was beginning to look anxious. 'Just an X-ray to begin with, and then I want you to come back here and I'll talk to you again.' To Sam, she said, 'A lady will take a picture of your chest, so that we can see what it looks like inside. You won't feel a thing, I promise.'

She wrote out an X-ray form and handed it to his mother. 'Take Sam along to the X-ray department now. They should be able to fit you in some time in the next half-hour. Come back here when you've finished, and tell the nurse that you're waiting to see me.'

Katie pulled back the curtain of the cubicle a moment or so later, and watched them leave. Drew was just coming out of his office and Craig was with him, looking tense. She would have spoken to him but he hurried away and she frowned.

Drew said, 'Did you examine the little boy?'

'Yes, I did.' She hesitated. 'I hope Craig isn't in any trouble.'

His mouth made a dismissive quirk, but he said, 'You're very fond of him, aren't you? You're always quick to rush to his defence.' He shook his head as though he was batting the thought away. 'I'm afraid you'll have to ask him, if you're concerned about his well-being. It isn't something that I would discuss with anybody else. What happens in my office is private. It's up to Craig if he wants to talk to you about it.'

She felt as though she'd been reprimanded. 'Yes, you're right, of course.'

'How did you get on with the little boy? Did you come to any conclusion about what's wrong with him?'

'Not yet. I need to do some tests.' She was quiet for a moment, and then said, 'Technically, his case wasn't an emergency. I doubt that anything untoward would have happened if he'd gone home.'

'It looked as though he was an emergency when he arrived. He had collapsed, and it was only because he'd had time to recover himself that it seemed like a simple faint.' He looked at her, his eyes dark and assessing. 'I think you should stop trying to protect your friend.'

She returned his stare. 'I'm just trying to put the record straight.'

'There's no need for you to do that. I asked you to

examine the boy. What do you think the problem might be?' He was being very cool and professional, and she felt uncomfortable. It was fairly obvious that Craig had made a misdiagnosis, and that was why Drew had asked to see him. She didn't want to get him into any trouble.

She said carefully, 'I thought I heard a heart murmur when I examined him. It wasn't very distinct and it could have easily been missed but, given the fainting episodes, I thought it ought to be investigated a little more.'

'What do you plan to do?'

'I've sent him for a chest X-ray, and as soon as he gets back I'm going to do an ECG.'

'What are you expecting to find?'

'I'm not sure yet. I suspect there may be some kind of valvular problem...perhaps an aortic stenosis. We'll need an echocardiogram to be sure.'

He nodded. 'If that's what you find, you had better refer him to a specialist. Make sure that he has antibiotic cover to prevent any infection of the valve, and explain to his mother what the treatment options might be. Otherwise she could worry unnecessarily.'

'I'll do that.' She hesitated once more, and then added, 'You know, Craig isn't feeling too well today. He mentioned that he had a cold coming on, and he may be a little deaf because of that. It would have been fairly easy to miss something under those circumstances.'

'If he isn't up to the job, he shouldn't be here.'

'And if he wasn't here, we'd be short-handed.'

'Better that than we miss something.' He started to move away from her. 'I have to go to a meeting. Let me know what happens with the boy.'

'I will.' She watched him walk away. It was unnerving having him so near and yet so distant in his manner.

He was gone for the rest of the morning and Katie fretted, feeling out of sorts and nervy. How she was going to go on working with him? It was proving more difficult than she had expected, and she was torn by the constant see-sawing of her emotions.

She spent her lunch-break with Becky. 'How are you feeling?' she asked. Becky looked very pale, her fair hair accentuating her pallor, and her blue eyes were shadowed. Katie guessed that she was anaemic.

'I'm all right really. I feel such a fraud lying here when I should be at home, looking after Reece.'

Katie shook her head. 'You wouldn't be here if it wasn't important that you get the rest. I imagine the doctors are worried about both you and the baby, and they'll only let you go home when they feel that you are OK.'

Becky nodded, looking forlorn. 'They say my blood pressure is coming down, but they need it to stay down, and they want to make sure that I'm not anaemic.' She frowned. 'Tell me about Reece. How is he doing? I wish I could see him.'

'He's settled down, and he seems to be getting used to staying with me. He knows that it's only for a short time and he wants to come and see you. Do you think you'll feel well enough if I bring him in to see you later today?'

Becky brightened. 'Would you? I would love that. Luke has been so protective—I don't think he realises how much I miss him.'

'I'll bring him in after I finish work…just for a few minutes, mind. I don't want the nurses telling me off.'

Becky was much happier by the time Katie had to leave, and she was overjoyed when Katie brought Reece to the ward later on. Reece showed her a picture he had made for her, and presented her with a bunch of flowers that he had gathered from Katie's garden. There were roses and brightly coloured petunias, and mixed in among them were buttercups and daisies and the odd sprig of clover.

'These are the most beautiful flowers I've ever been given,' Becky told him, and Reece beamed with pleasure.

'Auntie Katie said we could plant some seeds in the garden and grow some more,' he said eagerly. 'We've dug a little patch in a corner, and I've raked it over to get it ready.' He looked at his mother, his eyes shining. 'When you come out of hospital you can come and look at it.'

'I'll look forward to that,' Becky said with a smile.

When Katie took him home, he was still buzzing with energy, and she sent him out into the garden to play while she got on with some chores in the kitchen.

She kept an eye on him through the window, and after a while she went out to join him.

'I'll go and get the garden tools,' she said, 'and we'll get started on planting the seeds.'

'OK.'

She went into the little potting shed and rummaged about. In the distance, she could hear a dog barking.

'Here we are,' she said, coming back out onto the path. 'You can make a little channel in the soil with your trowel.' She looked around, but Reece was no-where to be seen.

Dismayed, she searched the garden for him. Perhaps he was hiding in the shrubbery. When she looked there, there was no sign of him. Her glance went to the fence. Had he gone through the gap? She had thought it just a small hole, but perhaps it was big enough for him to squeeze through.

'Reece,' she called. 'Where are you?' There was no answer and she began to panic. 'Reece,' she called again. 'I need you to tell me where you are.'

There was still no answer, and she ran to the gate and unbolted it, hurrying out onto the strip of meadowland that backed onto her garden. Where on earth could he be?

'Reece, you must answer me. I'm not playing hide and seek. Tell me where you are.'

After a few more minutes of desperately searching for him, she heard the sound of breaking glass coming from the direction of her old family home. The house and gardens were surrounded by a hedge, but there was a break in the greenery and she squeezed her way through, still calling out Reece's name.

It was a long garden, divided into different areas, one for rows of vegetables, another for a fruit garden, and beyond that, through an arched pergola, there was the main part, where in the time when her family had lived there there had been a lawn edged on all sides by curving flower borders. Perhaps it was still the same.

'What's the problem?' Drew came through the archway and walked towards her. 'I heard you shouting, and I heard the sound of glass breaking. Has something happened?'

Katie was relieved to see his tall, familiar figure. He looked so strong and confident, in control of himself, such a great contrast to her own sudden weakness.

'I've lost Reece,' she said shakily. 'I've been shouting his name, but he isn't answering. I can't see him anywhere.'

Drew glanced around the garden, his gaze moving over the fruit patch to the long line of canes, where runner bean plants curled up towards the sun.

'You think he must have come through here?'

She nodded. 'I can't think where else he would go. He can't get out onto the lane, and I wondered if he'd gone after your dog. I heard the dog bark.' She was confused. Bugsy didn't appear to be anywhere around.

'He was foraging around in the shrubbery a few minutes ago,' Drew murmured, 'but then he went racing off. I was just going to look for him.' He frowned. 'The greenhouse is still intact, so the sound of the glass breaking couldn't have come from there. Let's go and check the summerhouse.'

She followed him. He led the way through a thicket of trees, along a winding path, which was unfamiliar to her. It ended at a small rockery, where there were steps and a low wall and a raised area that overlooked a pond.

'Oh, no.' Katie pulled in a sharp breath. 'Please, don't tell me that he's gone in there.' Her voice was rising, wavering as she choked back her fears.

Drew turned and sent a fleeting glance over her. 'He's not in there.' He came towards her and put an arm around her. 'You mustn't think the worst. I'm sure we'll find him soon. We just have to keep looking.'

'It's all my fault. I turned my back for a minute and now I don't know what's happened to him. What am I going to do?'

'Call him again.'

She nodded. 'Reece, please, answer me. I need to know where you are. I need to know that you're safe.'

They waited and listened, but there was no sight or sound of him. Katie felt the blood draining from her face. How could she have been so negligent? If anything happened to him...

Drew's arms went around her. 'We'll find him.

You must believe that.' He held her, cradling her head against his chest, stroking the silky tendrils of her hair. 'He can't have gone far away.'

She tried to pull herself together, straightening up, and Drew loosened his grip on her, his hand sliding up to her shoulders, his thumbs gently kneading her tender flesh. 'Are you ready to go on?'

She nodded. 'Where is this summerhouse that you mentioned?'

'It's on the other side of the shrub garden. I had it placed there because that's where it gets full sun.'

They went around the shrubbery and Drew held onto her hand. His grasp was reassuring, strong and warm, and she was glad that she was not alone.

The summerhouse had double doors made up of small panes of glass, and there were windows at each side of the doors. One of them was opened to let in the air, and a couple of the panes of glass were broken. In front, there was a veranda, and there were tubs of flowers on either side. One of the tubs had tipped over, and there was a smattering of glass beside it on the wooden slats of the veranda floor.

As they walked over to the summerhouse, Bugsy came from around the side, tail wagging and his tongue lolling as he panted a greeting.

'What's going on, Bugsy? What have you been up to? Is this your handiwork?' Drew stared around him, a puzzled expression on his face. 'Or did the little boy do this?'

Clearly he didn't expect the dog to answer, but as

he went quietly around the summerhouse he was saying softly, 'I expect it was an accident. I'm sure he didn't mean to do any harm.'

There was a muffled sound, and Katie tensed. Was Reece around the back of the summerhouse? Was he hiding from them?

'It's all right, Reece,' she said gently, hoping that he was listening. 'I'm not cross with you. I just want to know that you're safe.'

She edged around the building and peered into the shadowy hedge at its back. A huddled little figure tried to make itself smaller.

'Reece, is that you?'

'No. He isn't here,' a small voice muttered, and Katie smiled, relief flooding through her.

'Are you sure?' she murmured. 'I really want to see him, and give him a cuddle, and make sure that he's safe.'

'I didn't mean to do it,' he mumbled into his T-shirt. 'It was a accident.'

'I know.' She moved towards him, and held out her arms. 'Come to me. Let's get you out of here.'

Slowly he shifted position, and she managed to slide her arms around him and draw him to her. 'Let's get you out into the open, where I can look at you.'

'I just wanted to see the doggy,' he said tearfully. 'I didn't mean to break the flowers.' He looked at Drew with a wary expression. 'Is you mad at me?' He huddled closer to Katie.

Drew went down on his haunches, facing Reece.

'No, of course I'm not mad at you. What happened? Were you trying to run away from me?'

'I came to see the doggy,' Reece said again, in a diffident tone. 'I didn't know you was here.'

'So you tried to climb on the tub and get into the summerhouse through the window?' Drew guessed.

Reece nodded. 'But I felled over.'

Katie looked at him. 'Are you hurt? Let me look at your arms and legs.'

He seemed to be all right, except for a graze on his leg. He stared at it, and his face crumpled. 'Me got blood, me got blood,' he cried, his voice rising in a shaky crescendo.

Drew said softly, 'I think we'd better get you into the house and clean you up a bit. Don't worry—it's nothing to worry about. You'll be fine. We'll look after you.'

He glanced at Katie. 'Shall I carry him into the house?'

She shook her head. 'I'll carry him. I think he's troubled enough at the moment.'

'OK.' He turned and called to the dog. 'Come on, Bugsy. We'd better get you inside, too.'

It was strange, going into the house where she had grown up. It had been several years now since she had lived here, and as she walked into the kitchen all the memories came rushing back.

She stood for a moment and stayed very still, gazing around at the big old stove and the oak kitchen units.

Drew must have been watching her because he said quietly, 'I expect it has changed quite a bit since you lived here. I haven't done much to it, but the previous owners did quite a lot of work. Mostly renovations, I think.'

She nodded, but she was too full of emotion for the moment to talk. Drew said, 'Come and settle Reece down in a chair by the table and I'll get the first-aid box.'

Katie realised that she couldn't stand there for ever and she began to move, stiffly at first, towards the table that was positioned to one side of the room. Reece was very quiet, wide-eyed, taking in everything around him. The dog moved around the kitchen joyfully, his tail wafting them as he passed by. He found his drinking bowl in one corner and started to lap noisily at the water.

Reece giggled. 'He's getting water everywhere,' he said gleefully.

Drew nodded. 'He does that.'

He squatted down beside Reece. 'Will you let me clean your cut? I'll be very gentle, I promise. When I'm sure that it doesn't have any dirt in it or any glass, I'll put a plaster on your leg. If you're very good,' he added, 'I'll see if I can find you some cookies.' He studied the boy for a moment. 'You do like cookies, don't you? I know your auntie likes them, because she always used to pinch mine when we were younger.'

Katie felt a swirl of hot remembrance glide through

her. It had been a teenage thing, a teasing battle between the two of them, and he had kept the memory, even after all these years...

Reece nodded, his eyes growing large and round, but he didn't answer. Katie was amazed that he sat and let Drew tend to his cuts. She had expected a battle, and tears, but there was none of that.

Drew was infinitely gentle, and when he had finished, true to his word, he fetched the cookie jar and let Reece help himself.

Katie murmured, 'I'm sorry about the damage to the summerhouse window. You must let me know how much it costs to repair it, and I'll write you a cheque.'

Drew shook his head. 'There's no need for you to do that. Forget about it.' He glanced at her. 'Now that you're here, would you like to see around the house, to see what changes have been made?'

Katie swallowed hard. It was a painful decision to make in a way. Part of her wanted to turn and run, but another part of her found it difficult to resist. This was the place where she had been born, where her family had lived for generations, and she was drawn by an inexplicable urge to explore.

She nodded. Turning to Reece, she held out her hand and said, 'Let's go and look around, shall we?'

Reece crinkled his nose. 'Me play with doggy. I want stay here.'

'I don't know about that,' she demurred. 'I'm not sure that I can trust you not to run away again.'

'I won't go away. I'll stay here.' He looked at her, his expression open and honest. 'Can I play with the doggy?' He looked from Katie to Drew, his eyes pleading with them to say yes.

'I don't think he'll run away again,' Reece said. 'I think he'll be all right here in the kitchen just for a minute or two.'

Katie relented. 'All right, then, but you must promise me, Reece, that you won't go out of the house.'

'I won't.' He turned to the dog and put his arms around Bugsy's neck. 'You and me play,' he said. Bugsy must have agreed with that plan of action because his tail began to wag vigorously.

'He'll be safe with Bugsy,' Drew said. 'He's wonderful with children, and we'll always be within shouting distance.'

'Just a quick look around, then,' she conceded doubtfully. 'Perhaps we'd better just stick to the ground floor. I don't want to be far away from Reece, and I want to keep an eye on him.'

He led her out of the kitchen. 'We'll start with the living room, shall we?'

She nodded. She could still keep Reece in view from here, through an archway and an inner feature wall of exquisitely decorated glass, and she was reassured enough to look around.

It was very much as she remembered. The people who had bought the house from her father had obviously cherished it. Some of the windows had been lovingly restored, and the huge fireplace in the living room had been renovated and brought back to its former glory.

'I used to love this room,' Katie murmured. 'I would curl up in the window-seat and look out over the lawn. It always seemed so big and rambling to me. I could have sat there for hours, dreaming my dreams.' She looked around once more, taking everything in. 'My grandmother would spend hours in the kitchen, baking, and the whole house would be filled with the smell of fresh baked bread. We'd sit in the dining room and bite into home-made bread spread with thick, creamy butter and topped off with her strawberry jam.' She smiled. 'We couldn't possibly do that nowadays, could we, with all the worries about cholesterol and so on?'

Her smile faded, and a fleeting look of sadness crossed her face. That was all in the past. She had to move on.

'I'm glad that you haven't made many changes,' she said. 'It all looks very much as it used to.'

'I'm glad about that. I wasn't sure how you would react.' He reached for her, running his hands along her arms in a gentle caress. 'I'm sorry if I hurt you by buying this house,' he said. 'It's the last thing in the world that I would want to do. I just didn't want to see it go to someone else…to a stranger.'

She returned his gaze, and in that moment she felt as though she was drowning in the deep dark waters of his eyes. He seemed to move towards her, slowly, but as though something compelled him, and in the next instant his lips were brushing hers tentatively, exploring the soft contours of her mouth, and then with a soft sigh he kissed her.

She gave herself up to that kiss. Everything in her being told her that it shouldn't be happening, but her heart wasn't listening. All that mattered was that he was holding her, that he was kissing her as though he couldn't help himself. Her body seemed to mesh with his, and the kiss tantalised and bewitched her. She lost all sense of time and place, and it was only when she heard an odd thud and Reece's piping voice in the distance that she came to her senses.

Tremulously, she pulled back from Drew. He was still holding her, but now it was at arm's length and she twisted around, looking in the direction of the sound that had interrupted them.

'Auntie Katie...Auntie Katie...' It wasn't an urgent cry, or a shocked cry, just a demand for attention, but it was enough to alert her to a new situation.

'I'm here, Reece,' she said. She broke away from Drew as though he was giving off an electric charge. She gave him a distracted look. 'I have to go.' She was shaking inside, confused about what had just happened and unable to think straight. 'I should take him home. It's very near his bedtime.'

'If you say so.' Reluctantly, Drew let her go and she hurried away to go in search of Reece. She found him in the utility room, just off the kitchen. 'What's wrong?' She glanced around and saw that he was standing in a corner, his thumb in his mouth. A box of detergent lay on the floor, the contents spilt out over the tiles.

'Wasn't me,' he said. 'It was the doggy's tail what done it.'

'I'll clear it up,' she said flatly, 'and then we should go home. It's getting very late.'

Drew had followed her into the room. 'I shouldn't have left it out on the low shelf,' he said. 'Don't worry about it. I'll clear it up later.' He glanced at Katie. 'If you're sure you must go, I'll see you both back to the cottage.'

Relieved that he wasn't in any trouble, Reece patted the dog's head and held Katie's hand. 'Is my daddy coming to fetch me tomorrow?'

'Yes,' Katie answered. 'He said he would take you to see Mummy.'

'Good.' Reece looked pleased, and Katie led him out of the house.

What would Luke's reaction be if he knew that she had been kissing Drew? She knew the answer. He would be horrified.

The three of them walked back to the cottage, and Katie ushered Reece into her small kitchen. She turned and gazed at Drew. 'I should get him to bed,' she muttered. 'Thank you for seeing us home. I'm sorry about the window and the mess in the utility room.' Her eyes were troubled, but she wasn't thinking about the mess. She was thinking that she should never have let herself get involved with him all over again. It would never work out.

He nodded, looking at her. 'I'll see you at work tomorrow?'

'Yes.' She ran the tip of her tongue lightly over her lower lip. 'About what happened...' she began, her glance darting to him and flicking away again.

'I know what you're going to say,' he said flatly. 'And you're right, I was out of order. It shouldn't have happened. I suppose I just wasn't thinking.' He moved away from the door and into the shadowy darkness outside. 'Put it out of your mind. I'll go now.'

He walked away, and Katie waited until there was no more sound of him and then she shut the door. She wished she knew what to do to put things right, but it wasn't going to be as easy to shut out the doubts that were crowding inside her head.

CHAPTER SIX

'WHAT happened with the little boy I treated yesterday?' Craig said. 'Dr Bradley asked you to take a look at him, didn't he?'

Katie nodded. She was writing up her notes, taking advantage of a few quiet moments in the department. 'You're talking about little Sam Slater, aren't you?'

'That's right. I thought he had a chest infection, and that he was anxious about school.'

'I had the results back this morning.' Her brow furrowed. 'He has an aortic stenosis. I imagine that he was born with it, but it didn't give him any symptoms until now.'

Craig winced. 'I should have picked up on it.' He sent her a worried glance. 'What's going to happen to him now?'

'I think the surgeon will try a valvuloplasty.'

'That's where they try to correct the narrowed heart valve by inserting a balloon catheter, isn't it?'

Katie nodded. 'When the balloon is inflated it helps to separate the flaps of the narrowed valve.'

Craig sighed. 'I think I'm in deep trouble with Drew Bradley. He thinks I'm too quick in my decisions.' He grimaced. 'I was really hoping that I would get better results on this posting. I wanted to apply for a place in a hospital nearer to where my parents live when my stint here is finished, but they have high standards there, and I don't think I'm going to make it.'

Katie's expression was subdued. 'Did Drew come up with any solutions? It couldn't have been all negative, could it?'

Craig shrugged negligently. 'He says I have to put in some extra study hours. He thinks I'm not paying enough attention to my studies.'

She glanced at him. He looked dejected, and she was sure he was losing weight. Was he ill? Was that why he wasn't coping? 'What are you going to do?'

'I don't see that I have many options. I'm going to have to do the extra work.'

Katie touched his hand with hers. 'Look on it as a way of benefiting yourself. We all have to go through these processes at some point. None of us are perfect.'

'I doubt you've ever had to do any extra studying. You always seemed pretty cool and collected to me, as though you have all the knowledge at your fingertips, without any hard slog.'

She made a face. 'Appearances can be deceptive. There are things I find difficult to deal with, problems I can't solve.'

'I find that hard to believe.' He picked up a chart and gave her an oblique glance. 'Anyway, it doesn't have to be work all the time, does it? We have to take some time out for relaxation. There's a film on at the local cinema—a real tear-jerker from what I've heard.

I wondered if you'd like to go and see it with me tomorrow? Your favourite actor is in it.'

'Thanks for the invitation, but perhaps some other time.'

'Yes. Some other time, then,' he said with a rueful smile. 'I'd better make a move. I can see Bradley is heading this way. I don't want him to think I'm slacking.'

Katie threw a quick glance in the direction of the automated doors. Drew was walking through the department, his stride purposeful and his manner confident.

She hadn't spoken to him since yesterday evening, and she felt awkward now, not knowing what she would say to him. She looked down at her notes and hoped that she looked as though she was engrossed in them. Perhaps he would pass her by.

'Did you find out whether James Mitchell's brother is around?' Drew asked, coming to stand alongside her. 'I've just been up to the ward to see how he's doing, and it's still looking pretty grim for him.'

'I think that welfare is still making enquiries. There might be a chance that he's working offshore, but it's taking a while for them to come up with anything certain.'

'At least you've had a result with the little boy with the heart problem.'

Katie was startled that he knew that. She frowned. 'I only heard this morning. How did you know about it?'

'I went and checked with the surgeon. I didn't think you would be far out on your diagnosis, and it seems that I was right.'

'Do you check up on all of your patients?'

He made a wry smile. 'Not all of them, or I would never get any work done. Little Sam Slater struck a chord with me, though.' He studied her thoughtfully. 'I'll come around and fix your fence for you. Will tomorrow evening be all right?'

'I don't want to put you to that trouble,' she said quickly. 'I can see to it, but I just need to organise a firm to come and do it. They're all a bit busy, and no one's given me a positive date for when they can do the work yet.'

'I'm not sure that it's a good idea to wait.' His eyes were dark, assessing her as he spoke. 'After all, if Reece can get through once, he can do it again.'

'I'm sorry about that.' Of course he didn't want people running all over his property. It was *his* property now after all. She said tautly, 'I'll keep him under a tighter rein from now on.'

'Don't worry about it. I have some wood, and it won't take me long to fix it.'

She nodded, giving in. If she wanted it done quickly, it seemed to be a simpler solution to let him do it. 'Tomorrow evening will be fine. I expect that I'll be at home, but if not, you can always let yourself in through the gate.'

'You won't be seeing Craig, then?'

Did he never miss anything? She evaded the question. 'It's been difficult for me to get out lately, now that I'm looking after Reece.'

'Can't his father have him at home with him sometimes?' Drew asked.

'Yes, of course. He sees him every day, but things have been difficult for him with Becky in hospital. He wants to be with her in the evenings. Perhaps, with a bit of luck, she'll improve enough to come home in a week or two.'

'I hope so. It must be very demanding for you these days, having to cope with coming to work and looking after a four-year-old. I'm not sure that it's something I would want to do.'

'Are you saying that you don't want children of your own some day?' It had never occurred to her that Drew might not want a family of his own.

'No, I'm not saying that. I suppose it's different with your own offspring, but you've been thrown in at the deep end, so to speak. That must be hard.'

'It's not so bad.' She didn't know how to cope when he was being sympathetic towards her. It was one thing to work with him and keep up a professional relationship, but it was quite another to balance the demands of heart and head. After what had happened last night, she felt awkward and out of her depth.

Across the room, she saw that Hannah was signalling to her. She said softly, 'There's another patient coming in. I need to prepare.'

Drew nodded obliquely and let her go, and while

Hannah was updating her on the forthcoming arrival, Katie saw that he was caught up in dealing with an emergency patient of his own.

'There's been an accident at the fairground,' Hannah told her. 'A boy of about twelve years old. They seem to think he was messing around with his safety belt and he was thrown off one of the rides.'

'There would have to be an investigation, surely?' It was horrifying to think that something like that could happen. 'How bad is it?'

'A head injury, we think, and possibly a fractured clavicle. The paramedics are bringing him in now. They expect to be here in five minutes.'

'I'll get ready,' Katie said. 'Are his parents coming in with him?'

'I don't think so,' Hannah said. 'It looks as though he was on his own. There may have been a friend, of course, so we may get some more information soon.'

When the boy was brought in on a trolley, he was barely conscious. Katie tried to speak to him but received little response. There was a nasty wound to his head, and it was bleeding profusely. The paramedics had placed a protective collar around his neck and he was being given oxygen.

'I'm going to put an IV in and send blood for cross-matching,' she told Hannah. 'He's hypotensive and his heart is racing, so we need to get some fluids into him, but we have to do that carefully so as not to cause any rise in intracranial pressure. He'll also need analgesia. I want to concentrate on stopping the haemorrhage. Just as soon as we have him stabilised we'll get an X-ray.'

They worked swiftly, but the boy began to convulse and Katie hurried to treat the fits with diazepam.

'They're coming under control, I think,' Hannah said.

Katie nodded. 'So far, so good. I'm going to give him a different medication to see if I can prevent any more from starting.'

She felt as though she was working against time, and when Hannah said urgently, 'His intracranial pressure seems to be rising,' Katie felt as though her efforts were in vain.

'You had better call the neurosurgeon and inform Paediatrics. There must be more going on here than we thought.'

'Are you coping here?' Drew was suddenly next to her and she felt a rush of relief course through her whole body. Drew would know what to do. She could rely on him to bring the most vulnerable patient back from the brink, and now that a child was involved she wanted all the help she could get.

'I'm worried about him,' she confessed. 'I need to get him to X-Ray, and his intracranial pressure's rising. I'm afraid that I'm losing the battle.'

'Try mannitol to buy some more time,' Drew said. 'It might stave off the worst, so that we can get him to X-Ray and up to neurosurgery. You could be dealing with a compound fracture and possibly a haematoma.'

Katie prepared the solution. 'OK, let's get him to X-Ray and find out what we're dealing with.'

Katie accompanied the boy to X-ray, and when they arrived back in the department she told Drew, 'You were right. It is a compound fracture, and the CT scan showed a blood clot forming. He needs to go for surgery right away.'

Drew nodded. 'The surgeon's ready for him.' He turned to Hannah. 'Do we have any idea where the parents are?'

'We're trying to contact them now. A friend turned up. He'd been hiding in case there was any trouble. According to the friend, the boy's name is Alex, and his parents are separated. He's been living with his mother, but the friend seemed to think Alex was running away to find his father. Apparently he left the house this morning without saying anything, and they hopped on a train to the next county. I suppose the friend thought it was some kind of adventure.'

Drew grimaced. 'That sounds like an almighty mess. I wonder if the friend's parents knew where their son was.'

'Probably not. The police are sorting it all out.' Katie supervised Alex's transfer to Theatre, and wondered how on earth she was going to explain to the parents what had happened to their son.

While she was waiting for the outcome of Alex's surgery, Katie saw several other patients. She was just finishing off suturing a nasty injury to a man's hand when Hannah approached.

'Is there news of Alex?' Katie asked.

Hannah shook her head. 'He's still in Theatre. I just came to tell you that a man is here, asking to see you. He says his name's Carl Mitchell.'

James Mitchell's brother. Katie stared at her. 'They managed to find him, then? Where is he?'

'I showed him into the relatives' waiting room.'

'I'll just finish these sutures and then I'll go and talk to him. Thanks, Hannah.'

Carl Mitchell was a big man, broad-shouldered, long-limbed, his complexion weathered by years of outdoor life. Katie greeted him warmly and said gently, 'I'm so glad that we managed to find you. Your brother had no idea where you might be.'

'I've been working on a fishing boat further up the coast.' He looked distracted. 'I haven't seen my brother for years.' He frowned. 'I was told that he was ill—that it was serious.'

Katie nodded. 'He was brought in the other day, and we did what we could for him. He's had sur- gery...' She looked at him anxiously. 'I'm not sure how much you've been told. His condition was very serious.'

'How bad is it?'

'He's very ill.' She hesitated, and then said, 'It's touch and go whether he will make it, I'm afraid.' She looked at him intently. 'Would you like to go and see him? He's on a ward and I can get someone to show you where he is.'

'I'm not sure that he would want to see me. Perhaps

it wouldn't be a very good idea. We had a bad argument some years ago and we haven't spoken since. We used to own a fishing boat together, and he wanted out and that left me in a difficult situation. We said things that perhaps we shouldn't have said, and we never made up. I told him that I never wanted to see him again. I feel bad about that now.' He pressed his lips together. 'I'm not sure that I can do this. He was very bitter about my reaction.'

'Will you be able to live with yourself if you don't? You're here now, and that must surely mean that you care about him. I think you need to take this opportunity to go and see him, for your own peace of mind.'

'Will he be able to talk to me? I don't want to make things worse for him.'

'He's conscious, so I'm sure he will know that you're there. I don't think you will be able to forgive yourself if you don't go and see him. You might not get the chance again.'

He looked as though he was turning it over in his mind, and Katie looked around for Hannah. 'Let me see if a nurse can find someone who will take you to him.'

A few minutes later a porter was showing him the way to the ward, and as he left the emergency department there was a flurry of activity and a man and a woman came hurrying through the double doors towards Reception.

'You can't go through there,' Katie heard the desk

clerk call out. She frowned, and looked over to where
the disruption was coming from.

'I want to see my boy. Where is he?' A man came
charging through the department and Katie moved towards him. The woman with him said tightly, 'You're
not going to do any good by shouting the odds.'

He ignored her and rushed forward. Katie said quietly, 'Would you like to tell me what the problem is?'

'You have my son in here. I was told Alex was
hurt and he was being operated on. What happened
to him? Where is he?'

'Are you Mr Daventry?'

He stared at her. 'Yes, I am. Who are you?'

'I'm Dr Sherbourn. I treated your son when he was
brought in here. Perhaps we could go somewhere and
talk privately?' She looked from him to the woman.
'Are you Mrs Daventry?'

The woman nodded. 'My husband and I are separated, but Alex is our son. I'm sorry about all this.
We're very worried.'

'I don't need you to apologise on my behalf,' Mr
Daventry bit out. His voice was raised and angry, and
Katie took a step backwards in alarm as he turned
towards her in an aggressive way. 'You say you were
the one who treated him—so tell me why he needed
an operation. He didn't need one when he came in.
They told me he banged his head. How could he end
up having to have surgery? Didn't you do your job
properly?'

Drew came forward and stood between them. 'I

think you need to calm down,' he said. 'Dr Sherbourn
has done everything possible to save your son. I understand that you're worried and upset, but we have
people here who are seriously ill and you're causing
a disturbance. If you go with Dr Sherbourn, she will
tell you what's happened to Alex.'

Drew went with them to the waiting room and
stayed while Katie explained Alex's condition to
them. He was watchful, and she wondered whether
he was reluctant to leave her with the threat of further
aggression. She was the doctor who had treated Alex,
though, and it was probably best that she was the one
to tell the parents what was wrong with him.

'He's in the recovery room at the moment,' she
said. 'You'll be able to see him just as soon as the
medical team feel he's stable enough.'

'I still don't see why he was operated on at all.'
Mr Daventry snapped. 'I didn't give permission. How
can you just go ahead without involving his parents?'

'We had no choice,' she said quietly. 'It was a life-
and-death situation, and we have a duty of care.'

'My husband's father died on the operating table,'
Mrs Daventry said in a quiet voice. 'He tries to avoid
hospitals wherever possible.'

'I don't need you to explain the way I feel,' her
husband said abruptly. 'That's my business and no
one else's. This is all your fault. If you had taken
proper care of Alex, he wouldn't have run away.' He
looked as though he was about to strike her, and Drew
moved towards him. Katie stepped back in alarm.

'You need to calm down if you want to see your son,' he said. 'Perhaps we can get you some tea, and you can wait in here while we find out how he's doing. As soon as we have any news, we'll come and let you know.'

'It's not good enough,' the man said. 'None of this should have happened. I hold the fairground responsible, and if anything happens to my boy while he's here, I'll sue the hospital.'

'That's your choice,' Drew commented. He turned to the woman. 'Can we get you anything? Would you like someone to come and sit with you and talk you through what's being done for Alex? I can ask one of the surgical team to come and explain things to you.'

'Thank you. Yes, I would appreciate that.'

Drew asked Katie to go and advise the surgical team that the parents were in the hospital, and she guessed that he was removing her from the scene. It was perhaps just as well, because she was feeling shaken up after the events of the day. It was difficult enough to deal with critically ill patients, but to be confronted with the threat of violence made matters much worse.

When she came back with the surgeon some minutes later, Drew had organised a tray of tea and biscuits and the man was more sober in his manner. Drew was good with people, Katie reflected. He knew how to defuse situations. She had seen him in action before, and she wished that he could show the same compassion in his dealings with Craig.

Alex was still in a bad way and Katie was distressed about that. The surgeon had managed to remove the clot, but now it was just a question of time to see whether the boy would pull through.

There was another shock waiting for her when she returned to the emergency room. Carl Mitchell was there and he looked terrible. His face was ashen.

'Did you see your brother?' Katie asked him.

He nodded. 'I was too late. He had slipped into a coma, and he didn't see me at all. He died just a few minutes ago.'

'I'm so sorry,' Katie said. She had such high hopes that he would come through the surgery and gradually recover, and now those hopes were dashed. She had raised Carl's hopes, too, and all for nothing. All their efforts had been for nothing.

'What do I do now?' he said. He answered his own question. 'I suppose I'd better arrange all the formalities. What a waste.'

Katie talked to him for a while, but there was nothing she could say that would take away the pain and sense of loss. Could she have done something more to save James Mitchell? Could this day get any worse?

She went over to the desk and started to write up some of her notes while there was a short break in the rush. Hannah was on the phone, and she turned to her now and said, 'Katie, it's your mother on the line. It sounds as if she's worried about something.'

'Mum,' Katie said. 'Is everything all right?' It wasn't like her mother to call her at work. She was always afraid that Katie would be in the middle of something and she didn't like to disturb her. That knowledge alone brought a tight feeling to Katie's stomach.

'It's your father,' her mother said. 'He's not looked right for ages now, and he's bruising all over, feeling nauseous. He doesn't complain, but I know that he's getting pains in his abdomen, and now he has a nose-bleed and it won't stop. I don't know what do. I'm sure the tablets he's on are causing this. What shall I do?'

'You need to bring him into the hospital, Mum,' Katie said quickly. 'It sounds as though the antico-agulation therapy needs to be stopped for a while so that we can get it down to the right level. If you bring him in, we'll do what we can to stop the bleeding. Can you get him here right away?'

'The car's at the garage, but I'll take a taxi. I'll be with you in a little while.'

Katie put down the receiver and pulled in a deep breath. Hannah was watching her, and she asked, 'Is there something wrong with your dad?'

Katie nodded. 'He's on medication to thin his blood, and it's doing it too well. He's been having problems with his heart rhythm, and he needed the therapy before he could have treatment to put it right.

This means that the treatment will be delayed even longer. He's such a stubborn man. I told him to go and see the specialist and get this sorted out.'

Hannah laid a hand lightly on her shoulder. 'At least now he can't give you any arguments. He has to get help.'

'I suppose you're right.' She went to prepare a treatment table for her father, setting out equipment in readiness for a slow intravenous administration of vitamin K. That should help to bring the bleeding under control. She would treat him herself and make arrangements for him to be admitted. She winced. He was bound to give her an argument about that.

'Hannah just told me about your father,' Drew said, coming over to her. 'Are you going to be all right, dealing with him? Do you want me to take over?'

'No, I'd better do it. I want to do it. Anyway,' she said with painful honesty, 'he won't want you to treat him.' She glanced up at him, her expression anguished. 'I know that's blunt, but it's the truth and there's no sense in hiding it. Even if we put aside what went on in the past, he's still very upset that your father has a contract here. He thinks he only got it because you put a word in for him.'

'My father's a good businessman. He always has been. He looks for opportunities and he gets in quickly whenever there's an opening. I can't blame him for that.'

'I've never known you to blame your father for

anything,' she said in a dry tone. 'You always take his side.'

'Why wouldn't I?' he said.

She made a wry smile. 'Well, there's the rub.' He hadn't denied that he had put a word in for his father but he hadn't admitted it either. She sent him a sideways look. 'It does seem odd that everything should come up roses for him every time. Don't you agree?'

'Am I being accused of something?' Drew returned her look, and his expression was dark and brooding.

'I haven't accused you of anything. I'm just saying that with the slightest effort, everything he touches goes well for him, whereas my father worked for years to build up his business, only to be thrown off the board without a by-your-leave. Now he has to struggle for everything, and it just isn't fair.' Her tone was sharp, more so than she had intended, and she bit her lip to stop herself from saying more.

'I'm sorry that you feel that way.' His mouth was straight, uncompromising. 'My father's had to work hard, too, though you may not believe that. There's no way I can help you if you go on ignoring that fact, and I'm not going to stand around here and argue the point with you.'

Stiffly, he moved away from her, and she felt the chill of the atmosphere waft and settle around her.

When her father came in a few minutes later, the sight of him shocked her. Blood was running from his nose, he was pale and breathless and his chest and arms were bruised from the effects of the medication. He looked dreadful.

'Oh, Dad, I wish you hadn't left things to get this far. I'm going to set up an intravenous line to give you the medication to stop the bleeding. We're going to have to admit you, so that we can monitor you while we get you off the anticoagulant therapy. Why did you let it come to this? I asked you to talk to the GP or the specialist.'

'I thought they'd make me come here,' he said with an effort, 'and this is the last place I want to be. It's bad enough that Becky's here.' He made a grimace. 'And now I'm going to be surrounded by Jacob Bradley's monitors. What an irony.'

'Try not to think about that,' she said. She was conscious of Drew, keeping a careful eye on them in the background. He must have heard what her father had said. 'I'm going to do what I can to look after you. I want you to concentrate on getting well again.'

'I'm glad that you're here, Katie. You're a breath of fresh air.'

Katie smiled. 'I'm going to get a nurse to come and help stop the bleeding. I just want you to try to relax.'

He was in a sorry state, getting weaker by the minute. She worked with her father for the next half-hour, and when she had done all that she could, she made arrangements for him to be admitted to a ward.

She turned to her mother, who had been hovering just a few feet away. 'You can go with him, Mum, and see him settled in. I'll drop by later on when my shift comes to an end.'

She watched him being wheeled away a little later, and she felt completely drained. Everything was going wrong today. The little boy was still critically ill, one of her patients had died and now her father was in dire straits. Her shoulders slumped. Why was this happening to her?

'You should go and take a break,' Drew said, passing by on his way to the light box to look at some X-rays. He scanned her features. 'You've had a lot to deal with today, and you need to take some time out. You could go and see your father on the ward if you like. We can cope down here.'

'Thanks,' she said, her voice a touch shaky. 'Yes, I will in a little while. It will take a half an hour or so for him to be settled on to the ward, so perhaps I'll go up when all the form-filling's been sorted out.'

'That's a good idea. Go and get yourself a coffee now in the doctors' lounge.'

She shook her head. 'There are still patients I need to see.'

Drew's mouth tightened. 'I wasn't making a suggestion. I was telling you how it's going to be. Someone else will deal with the patients.' He handed the X-rays to the desk clerk and asked him to put them in the filing tray. Then he took Katie purposefully by the arm and marched her towards the doctors' lounge. Pushing open the door, he urged her into the room.

'I said that you were to have a coffee,' he repeated. 'That was doctor's orders. You look as white as a sheet, and you're no good to anybody in that condition.'

He went over to the coffee-machine and poured coffee into two mugs. Handing one to her, he said, 'Drink. You'll feel better.' He wrapped her hands around the mug as though he didn't trust her to hold it steady, and the simple gesture threatened to undermine her already precarious self-control.

'I don't think anything will make me feel better today. I'm a terrible doctor. I can't get anything right. I can't even deal with patients' relatives.'

She sipped her coffee and then put the mug down on to a table. 'I don't know what I'm doing wrong. I just feel as though everything is falling down around me.'

He put his cup down and came over to her, looking her in the eyes. 'Try to look at this logically. You're tired and overwhelmed. You've been looking after Reece every evening and getting him ready for school in the morning, and that can't be easy when you're not used to it. Your sister-in-law's ill and now your father is, too, and your mother's upset. You're being much too hard on yourself.'

'I should be able to handle it.'

'You don't have to do it all on your own. You're only human, and you struggle along with the rest of us, and you shouldn't be afraid to ask for help when you need it. Just talking your problems through can help sometimes.'

His arms folded around her, and it was comforting, being held this way, feeling the steady beat of his heart beneath her cheek, allowing him to take some of the burden from her. She felt weak, and vulnerable, but now his strength was seeping into her with every passing moment and she leaned into him, craving his warmth.

'Katie? Let me help you. Let me take some of your troubles on my shoulders.'

She looked up at him, and her lips parted as she was trying to find the words to tell him how she felt. The next moment his head had lowered and his mouth was claiming hers, and his kiss was possessive and thorough, determined, as though he would sweep away all her doubts.

The floor seemed unsteady beneath her feet, as though the world was spinning around, but she was so glad that he was kissing her. She returned the kiss, her mouth softening against his, and she revelled in the joy of having his lips on hers. His hands stroked her, trailing over the curve of her hip, sliding across the small of her back, drawing her ever closer to him. She wished that she could merge into him, and that they could be as one...

'I'm glad you're here with me,' she mumbled. 'Things don't seem so bad when I know you're by my side.'

'We'll take good care of your father,' Drew muttered, looking down at her. 'He's in safe hands now. We'll monitor him all the time. That's all you need to think about.'

'We'll monitor him,' she echoed. Wasn't that what her father had said? He was surrounded by Jacob Bradley's equipment and that thought had clogged in his throat.

Katie tensed. What was she doing, drowning in Drew's embrace, taking comfort in the warmth of his caresses, when she knew in some far-off corner of her mind that this was all wrong, that nothing could ever come of it.

'I should go,' she said, her voice ragged. 'I need to go and see him.' She gazed around distractedly. 'I can't think straight in here.'

She took a step back from him. His arms were still around her, but she was distancing herself from him little by little. He loosened his hold on her gradually, his hands lightly curled around her arms as though he would put her away from him but couldn't quite bring himself to do it.

He drew in a deep breath. 'You're right. And I should get back to work,' he said. 'Drink your coffee. Take a few minutes. I don't want to see you back in A and E for a while.'

He released her, his eyes impenetrable, his features hardening, and when he turned away she wondered if he was remembering her accusations about his father. He walked towards the door and went out into the corridor without saying another word. It was what she had instigated, but she felt as though he had thrown cold water all over her.

CHAPTER SEVEN

'HAVE you seen Craig this morning?' Hannah asked with a frown. 'He should have been on duty an hour ago.'

Katie shook her head. 'I've been wondering what's happened to him myself. He could be ill, or just sleeping in late. I wasn't sure whether or not I should give him a ring, but to be honest I've been rushed off my feet and haven't really had a chance.'

Hannah made a face. 'I didn't think he looked too well yesterday, but it was hard to pin down what was wrong with him. He seemed a bit distracted, not quite on the ball, if you know what I mean. But, then again, he's been up and down a lot lately.'

'I do know what you mean.' She grimaced. 'If he doesn't come in to work soon, I think I'll phone him at home and see what's happening.' Like Hannah, she was concerned. If Craig was ill, they ought to be able to do something to help him.

'You don't actually look too good yourself,' Hannah said, giving her a quick look. 'Is anything wrong?'

Katie shook her head. 'I'm OK, really.' Drew had asked her that, too, earlier. She had worried that he would be offhand with her after what happened be-

tween them yesterday when her father had been admitted, but his manner had been perfectly normal towards her. His quiet concern had taken her off guard
and warmed her, and she held onto it, wrapping it
around her like a comfort blanket. 'I had a disturbed
night, that's all. Reece was a bit out of sorts, and
missing his mum…his dad, too. I think really he
ought to be staying with Luke because his whole
world is upside down just at the moment and he needs
a bit of stability, but Luke is still worried sick about
Becky and hardly able to concentrate.'

Perhaps she would have a word with Luke about
that. Becky seemed to be a improving now and the
baby she was expecting was doing well by all accounts. Perhaps Luke ought to be more watchful of
his son.

The double doors of the emergency department
swished open and Craig finally came in at a rush. He
was breathing fast as though he had been running,
and his hair was dishevelled as though he had been
raking his hands through it distractedly.

Katie hurried over to him. 'What happened?' she
asked. 'We've been worrying about you.'

Craig glanced at his reflection in a darkened window, pulled a comb from his pocket and ran it
through his hair. 'I didn't realise it was so late,' he
said. He checked his tongue in the makeshift mirror
and winced, pushing the comb back into his pocket.

A curtain swished open, and Drew appeared from
the cubicle where he had been treating a patient.

Craig's face fell, and Katie guessed that he had hoped his lateness hadn't been overlooked.

'So you're here at last,' Drew said, briskly. 'What kept you?'

'Sorry I'm late,' Craig answered. 'I had a bit of a stomach upset, but I'm all right now.'

'Are you sure?' Drew looked at him closely. 'You don't look too good. If you're not well, you should go home.'

It was true. Craig didn't look well, Katie thought. He was pale and there was a waxy sheen to his features that made her wonder what he had been going through.

'I'm fine now,' Craig said. 'It was just a meal that disagreed with me.'

Drew looked sceptical, but he said, 'That's good, but if you have any problems you should let me know. In the meantime, there's plenty to be getting on with. We've a patient coming in—a child with breathing problems. You can take that one. He'll be another fifteen minutes getting here, so you should just about have time to go and get yourself settled in.'

He turned to Katie and Hannah and indicated the cubicle he had come from. 'Will you give me a hand in here? I've managed to stabilise my patient's condition, but his pacemaker has malfunctioned and we need to be ready to act. Hannah, perhaps you could notify Cardiology.' He pulled back the curtain once more, and Katie hurried after him.

As soon as the cardiologist had made an appearance, Katie was able to attend to her own patients once more. Craig stopped her as she was on her way to deal with an arm fracture.

'The boy I'm treating looks to be suffering from croup,' he said. 'I've got him on humidified oxygen, but he isn't doing so well. I'm wondering if I should give him nebulised adrenaline. I can't get hold of Drew—he's treating someone and can't get away.'

'I'll come and take a look at the child. How old is he?'

'He's four years old.'

'Is he showing any signs of stridor or cyanosis?'

'Not so far.'

By now they had reached the cubicle where the four-year-old was being treated. His mother was by his side, and a nurse was watching over him. Katie introduced herself to the mother and the little boy, and swiftly examined him.

'You're doing very well, sweetheart,' she told the little boy, although she was worried about the pale tinge to his lips. 'The doctor is going to give you something to make you feel better and help you to breathe more easily.'

She moved away from the bedside and said quietly to Craig, 'Yes, you're right. It is croup. He's not doing too badly at the moment, but you should go ahead with the adrenaline. If his condition continues to deteriorate, follow the established procedures, in which case he'll probably need additional medication.' She went through the list of options, and then said, 'You need to work out the dosages carefully, to make sure that they're right for the child, but let me see your calculations before you give anything to him. You need to remember that there might be an airway obstruction. If he deteriorates, he'll need intubation, and we'll have to act quickly.'

Hannah caught up with her just then. 'Mrs Daventry is here, Katie. You remember the boy, Alex—the fairground head injury?'

Katie nodded. 'Yes, I remember him. He's still critically ill, isn't he?'

'Yes, he is. His mother's here and asking to see you. Can you spare her a few minutes?'

'Yes, I'll come and talk to her. Where is she? In the waiting room?'

Hannah nodded, and Katie turned to Craig and said, 'Come and find me if you need help.'

Hannah led the way to the waiting room, and Katie saw that Mrs Daventry was looking anxious. Hannah said, 'I'll go and get you a cup of tea, Mrs Daventry. Dr Sherbourn will have a word.'

'What can I do for you, Mrs Daventry?' Katie smiled a greeting. 'Is Alex no better?' The fact that they were rarely able to follow up on patients who had been admitted from A and E was one of the downsides of working here. Sometimes she managed to go and check up on what was happening, but there wasn't always the time. With Alex, though, she had made a special effort to go and see him at least once a day.

'He's conscious now,' the woman said. 'He came round a couple of hours ago. They say that's good, but he still looks terrible. Do you think he'll be all right? I don't know what to do. I don't know how to comfort him. He ran away because he wanted to find his father, and I don't know how to put things right. It's tearing him apart, us being separated, and I blame myself for what's happened.' She stopped talking, biting her lip. 'You were so good with him, and so kind, and I wanted to apologise for the way my husband spoke to you.'

'You don't need to apologise to me,' Katie said gently. 'When people are upset and worried, they sometimes do and say things that they regret later. We see a lot of it here when there's such a lot of stress to contend with. Don't let it trouble you.'

'That's very generous of you. My husband has a short fuse and it gets him into a lot of trouble. I think we could have made a go of it if it hadn't been for that. I sometimes think I ought to try again for Alex's sake, but I'm not sure if I can put myself through that any more.'

'I can't advise you what to do about your marriage,' Katie said quietly, 'but it seems to me that your husband might benefit from some counselling. Perhaps both of you would benefit. The first stop would be your GP.'

'Do you really think that's what I should try?' Mrs Daventry looked doubtful.

'It's up to you, of course. It's your decision, but in

your situation I would give it a go. As to Alex, I think he's probably very confused, and I wonder if you've sat down and talked with him about what's been going on.'

Mrs Daventry shook her head. 'You know, I don't think we did. We were so caught up in our own problems, so busy dealing with the immediate hassles, that we perhaps tended to overlook Alex's feelings in all this. Alex has always been a quiet boy, keeping things to himself, locked away inside him.' She gave Katie a quick smile. 'You've been a great help to me. You've given me some things to think about.'

Hannah came in with a cup of tea, and told Katie under her breath, 'I think you're needed back in the department. Craig could do with a helping hand.'

From the look of urgency in her eyes, Katie guessed that he was in trouble. She turned to Mrs Daventry. 'I'm afraid I have to go now, but perhaps Hannah will stay and talk to you for a while.' She sent Hannah a querying look, and Hannah nodded.

She hurried back to the emergency department. Something in Hannah's eyes had warned her that there was trouble brewing.

Craig was with the four-year-old boy, and he was preparing to administer medication. Katie glanced at the vial, and her eyes widened. Surely he wasn't going to go ahead without consulting someone? Or perhaps he had already had a word with Drew?

Even so, she couldn't see Drew condoning what he

was doing, and she said quickly, 'Dr Marshall. Can I interrupt you for a moment? I need a word, please.'

He stopped what he was doing and went with her to the desk. 'Is something wrong?'

'I saw the medication you were preparing. Have you checked the dosage of the drug you're about to give?' she queried.

'Of course I have,' he said with an air of nonchalance. 'It's the law to double-check all medication before it's given to a patient.' He frowned. 'I don't see what the problem is.'

'I told you to check with me,' she said, her mouth taut, certain that Craig wasn't being honest. 'I'm more used to dealing with paediatric cases than you are, and there are different concentrations of that medication. Your calculations may well have been accurate for the adult strength, but I don't think you've made allowances for the children's dosage. From what I could see you were going to give him too high a measure.'

Craig shook his head. 'It's not possible. I checked. I know what I'm doing.'

'Look again, Craig.'

He stared at her, then at the vial and the chart. After a moment he reeled backwards, his face deathly pale. 'I didn't know. I thought I had the right vial.'

'Perhaps you should have taken the day off after all,' Katie said with some sympathy. 'You didn't look well this morning, and you're obviously not thinking too clearly now.' Katie would have said something more, but Drew appeared out of nowhere and came over to them.

'Dr Marshall,' he said, 'could I have a word with you in my office?'

Craig opened his mouth and Drew added briskly, 'Now, if you please.' He glanced at Katie. 'Would you take over here? See to it that the little boy is tended to?'

Katie nodded. Craig still looked as though he was in a daze, but he went with Drew and the office door closed behind them. Katie stared at the door, wondering what on earth might be going on in there.

Hannah came over to the desk, looking worried. 'I'm sorry about that,' she said. 'I didn't know what to do. I could see what Craig was going to do and I tried to stop him, but he gave me an argument—said I was just a nurse and what did I know? Then Drew came and asked me what the problem was. I sort of hedged and Craig wandered off. I thought he was going to leave it alone, but obviously he changed his mind while I came to find you. I suppose Drew must have been keeping an eye on him, but then you came and intervened.'

'Oh, Lord.' Katie was torn between sympathy for Craig and exasperation. 'I don't know what's wrong with him, if he's not even listening to advice. I don't see how he can get over this one.'

She was worried about her own situation, too. Craig had come to her for help initially, and she didn't know whether Drew would blame her for not supervising him properly.

She went over it in her mind for the rest of the morning, but Drew didn't come near her and her patients kept her busy. In her lunch-break he was still nowhere to be seen and she escaped the turmoil of the department and went to visit Becky and then her father who was due back on the ward after having tests.

'How are you feeling now, Dad?' she asked, when he was settled on the ward once more. He looked awful, the strain of the last few days showing in his face, but at least he was being cared for, and she knew that it would take time for his new treatment to make a difference.

'I'm feeling a lot better, love,' he said. 'I feel a bit foolish, to tell you the truth. After all, you did warn me.'

'At least they're keeping a check on your heart condition while you're in here,' she said. 'That's good.' She gave him a look that was meant to be stern. 'It's time you were taken in hand.'

He chuckled, and it cheered her to see that he was at least in a good humour. 'Becky sends her love. She says we can't have both of you stuck in here, so one or other of you is going to have to make an effort to move.'

'That shows she's on the mend, doesn't it? Becky has a wry sense of humour.'

Katie chatted with him for a little while longer, but

she could see that he was getting more and more tired, and she glanced down at her watch. 'I have to go,' she said ruefully, 'but I'll come and see you again tomorrow. Behave yourself and do what the nurses tell you.'

She gave him a hug and went back to A and E. Drew was still occupied with an urgent case, and she went through the whole afternoon without crossing his path. Disappointment crowded in on her. She needed to see him, to talk to him, and the feeling was beginning to be like a hunger inside her. Craig wasn't anywhere to be seen, and she wondered if he'd been sent off duty.

When her shift came to an end, she went and collected Reece from her mother and then took him back to the cottage.

'Is my daddy coming today?' he asked.

'Yes, he said he would come and fetch you after you had your tea. He's going to take you to see Mummy.'

He smiled his satisfaction. 'Good. I'm going to play with my train now.'

'All right. Off you go.' She noticed that the dressing on his leg was getting a bit grubby. She would change it for him after tea. His leg was healing up after his accident with the glass, and it was lucky that it hadn't been more serious.

As she was getting the tea ready, she heard the doorbell ring. Reece was playing happily with his train set on the dining-room carpet, and she went to answer the front door. It was probably Luke, though he was early.

It wasn't Luke, though. Drew was standing in the porch and she saw that he was carrying planks of wood and a toolbox. His dog was with him, his tail making an exuberant swish, and now Bugsy bounded up to her, panting heavily. Smiling, she bent down and ruffled the puppy's head.

Drew said, 'I hope you don't mind me bringing Bugsy with me. I don't like to leave him on his own for too long.'

'No, of course I don't mind.' She looked up at him, and then at the dog, and then at the planks of wood. 'Oh,' she said. 'I'd forgotten all about the fence.' She went on looking at him, her heart thumping, drinking him in, and when he returned her gaze with a quizzical expression, she suddenly came to her senses and realised that she still hadn't invited him in. She stood back and waved a hand along the hallway, ushering him into the cottage.

'It shouldn't take me long to fix it,' he said. 'I'll go and get on with it right away.'

As he went through the kitchen, the water in the kettle began to boil and he said with a wry smile, 'Good. I could do with a cuppa.'

'Have you eaten?' she asked, and he shook his head.

'I haven't had time yet. I had to stay on at work to get a patient through a crisis, and then I decided

I'd better come and fix the fence before Reece went wandering again.'

He must have only stopped to change into casual clothes—black jeans and a loose shirt. He looked good, and she stared at him surreptitiously, appreciating what she saw, until she took herself in hand.

'I'll make you something,' she said. 'I was just making food for Reece and myself. You can join us if you like.'

'That sounds good to me.'

The dog disappeared into the dining room, and she made a quick check that all was well. Reece gave the dog a hug, and giggled when he knocked the train over with his tail.

'I think they'll be all right together,' she said, glancing at Drew. 'I can watch them from here while I finish off.'

He nodded. 'If you're sure, I'll go and get on.'

While he worked outside in the garden, she prepared a salad, and set the table with crusty bread and sliced meats. She could see him through the window, and there was something about the way he worked that made her feel wistful inside. His hands were strong and capable, competent in everything he did, and he made short work of the fence. In no time at all it seemed that he had removed the broken slats and secured new wood in their place.

He came back to the kitchen and put his toolbox down on the worktop. 'Is it all right if I wash up at the sink?'

She nodded. 'Of course.'

Bugsy came in from the dining room, his tail wagging, his face expectant, and Drew tickled his ears.

Reece followed the dog into the kitchen. 'I wish I had a doggy,' he said. 'I'm going to ask Daddy for one.'

Drew smiled at him. 'You and Bugsy seemed to get on well together. Even if your mum and dad won't let you have a dog, you can always play with Bugsy.' He glanced at Katie. 'If it's all right with your auntie, of course.'

Katie didn't answer for a moment. That would mean that Drew would be round here a lot, wouldn't it? A sensation of something warm and comforting curled inside her. She said quietly, 'That's fine by me.'

Drew washed at the sink, and she thought about what had happened earlier that day. She glanced at him, and quietly said what was on her mind. 'At work today—I've been thinking about what happened with Craig. I was supposed to be looking out for him. I was meant to be supervising him and then I was called away. I hope he isn't in too much trouble.'

Drew turned around from the sink and dried his hands on a towel. His jaw tensed. 'He knew that he should have asked for help, but he didn't. Yes, you were supervising him when I wasn't around, but you couldn't be there all the time. I don't see that you're to blame in any way.'

'What will happen to him?'

'I haven't decided yet. I'll have to keep an eye on things, and try to discover what's at the bottom of his problems. Off the record, if I can help him, I will, but the way he's going he needs to change his attitude.'

'You don't like him very much, do you?'

'It isn't a question of like or dislike. I'm responsible for what goes on in the department, and in the end I'm the one who has to take any flak. I can't just let him keep on making mistakes.'

'I heard that there was trouble with one of the doctors at the hospital where you worked before. He lost his job, didn't he? Weren't you behind his dismissal?'

'There were good reasons for what happened.' He looked at her, and his expression was suddenly unfathomable. 'Why are you asking?'

'I'm afraid that you might be too hard on Craig. I think he needs support, not censure.'

'And you think I'm not capable of being supportive?'

'I didn't say that.'

'You didn't need to. It's fairly clear that you take your opinion of me from what the rumour-mongers say.' He gave her an odd look. 'You don't know me very well, do you, Katie? We go way back, and yet sometimes I think you hardly know me at all.' He held her gaze steadily.

She pulled in a shaky breath. 'Did I touch a nerve?' She wasn't going to back down. 'Perhaps you're right. I may not know you as well as I thought I did.' She straightened her shoulders. 'Anyway,' she said, getting herself together, 'maybe this is the wrong time to be talking about any of this. I've made some food. It's the least I can do to thank you for mending the fence for me. Do you want to come and sit down and eat?'

He nodded. 'I won't say no. I'm famished, to be honest.'

It was a truce, of sorts. Drew sat and shared a meal with her and Reece, and the dog ate scraps from a bowl in the corner of the room. Reece was full of himself, telling Drew all about his train set and the way Bugsy kept getting in the way.

'Him sat on the truck.' He laughed and his eyes were wide and shining. 'It didn't break. Auntie Katie gave me the train set. It's well good.'

Drew laughed with him, and talked to him about nursery school and his friends until after a while Katie began to relax, too. When the meal was finished, she piled the dishes into the washing-up bowl and left them to soak. Reece went back into the dining room to play with his toys and the dog immediately followed him. They played together noisily.

Katie said musingly, 'You're very good with him. I haven't seen Reece so cheerful in a long while.'

'He's a lovely child,' Drew said, 'and he's very easy to get along with. Anyway, I think you've done a lot to make him feel more settled, given what's going on in his life at the moment.'

'I've done my best, but I'm only a stopgap, and there are times when he seems very vulnerable. All I can do then is to cuddle him and talk to him and try to show him that I care. It isn't always enough.'

He shook his head, coming over to her. 'You're much too hard on yourself,' he murmured. He drew her to him and kissed her lightly on the forehead. 'You've kept him safe and shown him that he's loved, and you can't do any more than that. He needs to be with his family, that's all.'

'You're being very understanding.' She made a faint smile. 'I don't deserve your support, but I don't know what I would do without it. Sometimes I feel so torn I don't know whether I'm coming or going.'

He looked into her eyes, and his expression was suddenly intent, warm and protective. 'I'll always be here for you, Katie. I want you to know that. I care about you. You've always been special to me.'

'Have I?' She returned his gaze, serious now, a flicker of hope growing inside her.

'You know you have. How can you doubt it?' His hand slowly stroked her spine, and came to rest in the small of her back. He lightly pulled her towards him. 'Even when you were just a teenager you lit up my life. I wanted to keep you safe, to treasure you and make the world a better place for you.'

Her mouth softened. 'And you did. You made me wish there was no one else around, only you and me, and the stars above us in the sky. They were our special light, casting a spell over us so that nothing could tear us apart.'

'I felt the same way. I wanted to wrap you up in

my arms and keep you with me for ever.' His lips brushed hers. 'You were so young, so beautiful. I didn't want anything to come between us.'

He kissed her, slowly, exploratively, his lips trailing fire over hers, his hands gliding over the softness of her curves and coming to rest on the gentle swell of one breast. The nub flowered and hardened with exquisite tension and she gave herself up to the kiss, melting against him as though all substance had gone and she was all pure, blissful sensation.

'I've wanted you so much,' she mumbled against his lips. 'I've missed you.'

'Me, too. I never wanted us to be apart. You were the only woman I ever wanted.' He kissed her again, and her whole body fizzed with exhilaration, the blood surging through her veins in a hot tide of yearning. She wanted more, much more than this.

Then there was a sudden loud clatter behind them, and the shock of the intrusion was so great that Katie broke away from Drew, her whole body trembling with alarm. What had just happened? Was it Reece? Was something wrong? But the sound had come from across the room, from the kitchen door, and Reece was in the opposite direction. A chill draught of air shivered past her shoulders.

'Am I disturbing something?' The voice was masculine, grim and edged with tart query. She looked towards the kitchen door and saw that her brother was standing there, an expression of caustic dislike on his face.

Reece came running in from the dining room. 'Daddy, Daddy,' he said eagerly. 'I been waiting for you.' He clasped his arms around his father's waist, and Bugsy came bounding in and tried to get in on the act.

Luke hugged his son and frowned at the dog. 'Is this the dog you were telling me about? He's the reason you got hurt the other day?'

'Bugsy didn't hurt me,' Reece said, his voice rising in astonishment. 'I climbed on the shed.' He stopped then, seeing his father's expression and obviously wondering if he was about to be in trouble once more. He stuck his thumb in his mouth. 'Didn't mean it,' he said, more hesitant now.

Luke stared across the room at Katie. 'You didn't hear me ring the doorbell or knock, so I let myself in. I had no idea that I would find you kissing the enemy. I thought you would have more sense.'

Drew said softly, 'I was just helping out with mending Katie's fence, that's all. She had a problem with some of the local tearaways, and some of the slats were broken, but it's all sorted now. The lads, too.'

'I suppose you think that's all that matters. Everything is water under the bridge to you, isn't it?' Luke's lip curled in an expression of contempt. 'I don't have any say over who my sister sees or doesn't see, but I don't want you around my boy. Stay away from us.'

'Luke, stop this. You've no right to say those

things to Drew.' She glanced at Reece, who was staring up at all of them in bewildered fashion. 'Besides,
you're upsetting Reece. You ought to know better
than that.'

Luke stared at her, his eyes as cold as ice. 'So had
you. I thought better of you, Katie.' He looked down
at Reece. 'Come on, son. Say goodbye to Auntie
Katie. We're going to see Mummy.'

Without another word he began to gather Reece's
things together and then headed for the door. At the
last moment he turned and said, 'Thanks for looking
after him, Katie, but I'll be keeping him with me from
now on. I won't be bringing him here again.'

He ushered Reece out of the door without a back-
ward glance. Reece craned his head around to look at
Katie, but his father tugged him away. 'Me want see
Auntie Katie,' Reece protested loudly. 'Me want see
Bugsy.'

Luke took no notice, but held onto his son's arm
and bundled him into his car. Katie hurried outside
and waved, blowing kisses at the little boy. 'Love
you,' she said, and he stared back miserably as the
car pulled away. She could see the tears glistening in
his eyes.

She felt as though her heart was being wrenched
from her. How could Luke do this to his child? How
could her own brother behave in such a callous fashion?

'He'll come around,' Drew said, coming alongside

her and helping her back to the house. 'He'll see sense once he's calmed down.'

Katie shook her head. 'No, he won't. This is Luke, this is my brother, and he can't see past the end of his nose. All he can see is that you and I are involved with each other, and he'll never forgive me for that.'

Her eyes shimmered with tears. 'I knew this would be a mistake. How could I ever have thought that I could simply forget my family and follow my heart? It will never work out…never.'

He held her to him, his arms wound tightly around her. She longed to bury her cheek against his chest and let him soothe away her fears, but that wasn't going to solve anything, was it? It would only make matters worse. If Luke came back—if he found that he had forgotten something—it would be disastrous for him to find Drew still here.

She rested a shaky hand against his rib cage, trying to put a little distance between them. 'Drew, I think perhaps you should go now,' she said in a choked voice. 'I need to be on my own for a while. I want some time to myself so that I can think things through.'

'That's not a good idea,' Drew murmured. 'I don't want to leave you on your own right now.'

'I know you don't, but you must,' she said, trying to inject a little firmness into her tone. 'My whole family is torn apart and I can't cope with any more now. I was wrong to think that things could ever be right for us.' She was afraid that she would break down in front of him, and then she would be totally lost.

'Couldn't you be open with your family? Tell them what you feel, so that we can have some kind of future together?'

She shook her head. 'They wouldn't accept it. You saw how Luke reacted.' Her voice broke on a sob. 'We don't have a future, you and I. It's impossible. There are too many barriers.'

Drew's mouth made a gesture of denial, but she flattened her hand on his chest and pushed him away.

'Please, go,' she said again, her voice a whisper now. She didn't look at him, but he must have finally accepted what she was saying because he released her and she was aware of him moving away from her.

There was a faint sound as he picked up his toolbox, and the knowledge that he had come here to help her made her feel all the more wretched. She heard him call to Bugsy and then he said quietly, 'I'll see you at work tomorrow. Call me if you need me. I'm only a short walk away.'

The door clicked shut behind him, and she went into the living room and sat down in the deep cushioned armchair, her body sapped of strength. She had known this would happen. From the moment he had come back into her life she had known, deep down, that her family would never tolerate her relationship with Drew. How was she ever to reconcile that with her feelings for him?

Seeing Reece's tearful expression had been the final straw. Was that the price she had to pay for loving Drew—to be cut off from her family, from those dearest to her, from the people who had nurtured her and loved her all her life? How could she ever come to terms with that?

CHAPTER EIGHT

'WHAT'S wrong, Mum?' Katie watched her mother move around the kitchen, briskly wiping down surfaces and pushing items out of her way with quick, impatient movements. When she came across one of Reece's toy cars, her mother frowned.

Katie was pretty sure that she knew what the problem was, but her mother hadn't given anything away so far, but maybe it was better brought out into the open. 'You're very quiet today and something's obviously on your mind.'

Her mother put the toy car up on a shelf. 'I think you know what's wrong, Katie. Luke came by and told me what happened the other day when he went to your house.' She pressed her lips together. 'It came as such a shock. I had no idea that you were involved with Drew in that way. I thought you would have more sense than that after what this family's been through.'

'It wasn't intentional.' Katie hesitated. 'Sometimes these things just happen...I didn't set out to hurt anyone, least of all you and Dad.'

'Your brother's very angry.'

'I know.' Sadness weighed her shoulders down. 'I hadn't expected him to react quite that way. I thought he would be upset perhaps…outraged even, but I never for one moment thought that he would take things so far. He hasn't let me anywhere near Reece these last few days. I've tried reasoning with him, but he won't listen.' She glanced across the table at her mother, her gaze troubled. 'Do you think he will come around eventually and change his mind?'

'Knowing Luke, I shouldn't think so. You know how he is. He digs his heels in and there's no moving him. And he's never forgiven the Bradleys for the way they've messed up his life. He feels that because they railroaded your dad into selling out, he's had to put aside his own career and take over the management of the company. He never wanted to do that.' She sighed and pushed back a soft tendril of auburn hair. 'You must have been mad to let yourself get into this situation. What were you thinking?'

'I wasn't thinking at all,' Katie admitted unhappily. She grimaced. 'He'll bring Reece here, though, won't he? Aren't you looking after him when you finish work in the afternoons? I'll be able to see him, then, when he's with you.'

'I wouldn't count on it. He's taken on a nanny to care for Reece while Becky's in hospital.' She pursed her lips. 'The way things are at the moment, he'd rather a total stranger took care of his lad than let you near him. He can't accept that you have anything at all to do with Drew outside work.'

'It wasn't Drew's fault that his father acted the way he did.'

'He supported him, though, and he doesn't seem to care about our feelings. He's even gone as far as buying the house that used to be ours when he knew how much we treasured it.' Her expression was angry, tight-lipped. 'I'd call that rubbing it in, wouldn't you?'

'I can't believe that he meant to hurt us. I think you're both forgetting a major fact here... Dad was paid for letting the company go. It wasn't Jacob Bradley who caused his downward spiral, but Dad's poor health. If he hadn't taken ill, he would have been able to cope with everything and make a success of things. I don't see how Drew can be blamed because things went wrong.'

'That's just the point, isn't it?' Her mother's voice was rising in renewed dissatisfaction. 'It was all the worry and stress of what happened that made him ill in the first place, and things are even worse now. How do you think your dad feels, knowing that you and Drew have something going? I'll tell you how he feels—let down, disappointed and deeply hurt. This isn't doing him any good at all.' Her face tightened. 'He's only been out of hospital for a day or so, and now it's as though he's gone back to square one. All this upset is having a terrible effect on his health. His heart rate's chaotic, all over the place, and he looks ashen.'

Alarmed, Katie said, 'I'll go and see him. He's upstairs, isn't he?'

She started for the door, and she was in the hallway

when her mother stopped her, saying abruptly, 'No, you won't. He's having a lie down and I won't have him disturbed all over again. The doctor's been in to see him and he says he needs to rest. I won't have you stirring things up and giving him a heart attack.'

Katie's eyes widened. 'I wouldn't do that…'

'I know you won't. I'm not giving you the chance. You've done enough damage already.'

'Mum, that's not fair.' Katie's voice broke. 'How can you say that to me?'

'Amy…' Her father's voice came from the bedroom upstairs, and Katie froze. 'Amy, what's happening? Who's there?'

Her mother called back, 'No one, dear. It's nothing for you to bother about.' She glanced at Katie and said in a low voice, 'You'd better go. I don't want him to find you here.'

Katie looked at her in shock. 'But he's my father, and he's ill. I need to know that he's all right.' Her mother's face was unyielding, though, and she added on a desperate note, 'I love you both dearly, and I never wanted to see you hurt. You have to believe me.'

'You should have thought about that before you got yourself involved with Drew,' her mother said in a harsh whisper. 'How did you expect us to feel?' She shook her head. 'You should go now, before he takes it into his head to come downstairs.'

She meant what she said, and Katie could see no other way but to leave. It broke her heart to go this way, like an outcast, rejected by her own family. Tears burned her eyes and she blinked them away, going out to her car and sitting in the driver's seat until she had herself under a semblance of control. It was her worst nightmare.

At work, too, over the next few days, Drew was remote, his manner professional and calm but nothing more. There was no friendly warmth, no attempt to stop and talk about anything other than the job in hand. It was as though he was distancing himself from her.

She concentrated all her attention on her work. It helped to blot everything out so that all she felt was numbness, and if her colleagues noticed that something was wrong, they soon stopped asking when she answered them with vague denials. Hannah was the only one who persisted.

'If you need someone to talk to, you know that I'm here,' she said softly. 'I don't know what's troubling you, but I know that something's not right, and if I can help in any way, you only have to ask.'

'Thanks. I'm fine.' Katie picked up a chart and scanned the details of her patient. 'Have you seen Craig around at all today? He should have been on duty yesterday, but he didn't show up. I wanted to check some lab results with him.'

Hannah shook her head. 'I haven't seen him since three or four days ago when you were off duty. He was grabbing things out of his locker and he said that he'd been told to take some time off. He seemed angry and resentful and he said that Drew had it in for him. I don't know what's been happening, but he seems to think he's under threat of dismissal, and he muttered something about Drew never liked him and that he's a control freak, someone who needs to show that he's in charge.'

Hannah grimaced. 'He was really hot under the collar. He said Drew had been responsible for getting a doctor dismissed from a job at another hospital, and I think he was making out that this was the same kind of thing. Do you have any idea what's been going on?'

Katie's brows drew together. 'I don't. No one has said anything to me.' She paused, thinking things through for a moment or two. 'I don't think Drew would behave in any way that was unfair. He's always been evenhanded and discreet in the way he handles work issues. I just can't see him letting his personal feelings come into it and override his judgement. There must be more to it than we know.'

Hannah nodded. 'I thought so, too.' She turned away and went back to work, and Katie started to head back to her patient, but almost ran into Drew as he approached the desk.

She stared up at him. How much had he heard?

He guessed what she was thinking. 'I couldn't help hearing some of what you said,' he murmured. 'I'm glad you didn't go along with the rumours that are flying around. Thank you for that.' A faint smile hovered about his lips. 'It's good to know that you have some faith in me.'

She frowned. What did he mean by that? Ignoring his words for the moment, she said, 'I know there have been problems between the two of you. I just don't accept that you would ever let them get in the way of your professional judgement.'

'You're right. I wouldn't. I'm aware that Craig has difficulties in some areas, and he needs a lot of support, but I've done my level best to help him. He just doesn't seem to want to co-operate with me.'

Katie nodded. 'He can be stubborn at times and a little arrogant. I'm worried about him, though. He's changed over these last few months, and he hasn't looked well for some time. I really feel that I ought to go and check on him.'

'Don't you have enough on your plate right now?'

She sent him a guarded look. 'You mean with my family?'

'That's right. I know it can't be easy for you.' His gaze meshed with hers and she was the one to look away.

'I can't do anything to put that right, but at least I can try to help Craig if he's in trouble. I know he lives in a flat near the hospital, so I thought I might go and check on him when I finish work.'

'Would you mind if I came with you?' She sent him a startled look and he added, 'I'm concerned about him, too. If he's all right, that's fine, and I'll just leave and go on my way, but I've a feeling that something's wrong.'

'Yes, of course you can come with me.' She stared at him. 'Why are you concerned?'

'I'd prefer to keep that to myself for now.' His gaze met hers. 'Are you off in an hour?'

She nodded, and he said, 'I'll meet you at the ambulance bay.'

Katie met him there as arranged as soon as she finished her shift. She wasn't sure whether it was a good idea to have Drew go with her or not, but at least he was talking to her again.

He was carrying a holdall, and she wondered what was in it, but other things were uppermost in her mind and she didn't ask.

Craig's flat was on the upper floor of a house that was part of a modest, neat terrace, fronted by wrought-iron railings and opening out onto the street from a set of steps. As Katie and Drew arrived there, a man from the ground-floor flat was just leaving.

Drew said quickly, 'We're looking for Craig Marshall. We both work with him at the hospital, but we haven't seen anything of him for a few days and we're wondering if he's all right. Have you seen anything of him?'

The young man shook his head. 'Can't say that I have. Not since a couple of days ago anyway. He came home and shut himself in his flat, and he doesn't seem to have come out since then. I heard him moving about in there a few hours ago, so I guess he's

all right. I would have heard the front door bang if
he had gone out.' He held open the main door. 'Go
on in and see for yourself. His flat's upstairs, and
you'll see his door just off the landing to the right.'

'Thanks.' They went up the stairs, and Katie
knocked on the door. After a moment or two, when
there was no answer, she knocked again and called
Craig's name.

'Are you in there? Craig, it's Katie. Will you let
me in?'

There was still no sign of him coming to the door
and she sent Drew an anxious look. 'What do we do
now? We've made enough noise to wake him if he
was asleep.'

'I'll break the door down.' He put the holdall on
to the floor.

She looked at him in alarm. 'Do you think you
should do that? What if he's just gone out for a while?
He's going to be pretty angry if we wreck his door,
isn't he?'

'You heard what the other tenant said. Don't worry
about it. I'll square it with him. Let's hope he hasn't
barricaded himself in with any super-strong bolts.'

He didn't give her time to voice any more objec-
tions, but applied his weight to the door, first with his
shoulder and then following that up with a hefty kick.
The lock caved in under the pressure, and the door
swung open.

Katie was shocked as she stepped inside the flat
and looked around. The curtains were drawn and ev-

erywhere was shrouded in darkness until Drew snapped on the light.

She blinked and looked around. Craig obviously hadn't bothered to tidy up in a long time, and there were piles of papers, dirty coffee-cups and the foil wrappers of take-away meals littering the table and cupboard tops. An air of neglect hung about the place, and she swallowed hard, worried about what she would find as she explored the rooms. Drew went to check out the bathroom and kitchen.

Craig was in the bedroom, and as soon as she saw him, Katie pulled in a shaky breath. 'Drew, I think you need to come here,' she called. Craig was sprawled across the bed, and beside him on the bedside table there was a bottle of tablets.

She leaned over Craig's prone form and called his name, but he didn't answer, and even when she gently shook him, there was still no response.

Drew came from the bathroom and raked a swift glance over him. 'Is he breathing?'

She nodded. 'He's in a really bad way, though. His heart rate is way too fast, and he feels hot to the touch. We should get him to hospital.'

Drew pulled his phone from his pocket and began dialling the emergency number. 'What are the tablets he was taking?'

'Amphetamines.' Katie turned back to Craig and checked his pulse once more. 'I don't think this was an intentional overdose, because there are still some tablets left in the bottle.' She winced. 'No wonder his

behaviour has been so erratic just lately. He must
have been trying to burn the candle both ends and
kept himself going by popping pills.'

Drew nodded, and just then Craig started to convulse. 'I brought some medical supplies with me in
the holdall,' Drew said. 'See if you can cool him
down with a cold flannel from the bathroom while I
get the diazepam from my bag. He'll need a beta-
blocker for the tachycardia.'

By the time the ambulance arrived, Craig had
stopped convulsing but his heart rate was still fast and
his temperature was still way too high. Katie insisted
on going with him in the ambulance. Drew followed
in his car.

Once at the hospital, they relinquished Craig to the
medical team on duty. Katie watched as her fellow
doctors worked on him, protecting his airway and giving him activated charcoal.

It was some time before a nurse came over to them.
She said quietly, 'We're doing what we can to get
the drug out of his system. His heart rate is beginning
to settle down, and his temperature is slowly drop-
ping. Those are both good signs.'

'Thank you.' Katie breathed a sigh of relief.

'He seems to be improving little by little,' Drew
murmured, standing beside her. 'I think we were
lucky in that we found him before things had gone
too far. Otherwise the outcome could have been much
worse.'

She sent him a sideways glance. 'You must have

been half expecting something like this. That's why you filled the holdall up with anything that you might need, wasn't it? How long have you known what he was doing?'

'I suspected he was taking drugs some weeks ago, but I couldn't be sure. Then I caught him in the act while he was on duty, and I had no choice but to suspend him. I wanted to do what I could to help him, and I offered him the chance to join a rehabilitation programme, but he refused. Even knowing that it could be the end of his career, he wouldn't see sense. He seemed to be in denial.'

'Did you threaten him with dismissal?'

'When he refused any kind of help, I realised that all I could do for the moment was to give him time to consider his options. He was supposed to get back to me by this morning.' His mouth made a rueful quirk. 'When he didn't do that, I decided I should go and see him for myself. I'm glad that I did.'

'So am I.' She slanted him a quick, oblique glance. 'Does this mean that it's all over for him now?' It would be such a waste of a once bright, intelligent man, who had such a lot to offer if only he could break the habit.

Drew shook his head. 'It's up to him. I'll put him on sick leave and have him admitted to the rehab ward, and hope that they can persuade him to see sense. He can dig himself out of this hole if he's determined enough, and if we back him up as much as we can, we might just be able to rescue his career.

I've been there before with another young doctor who was in trouble, and in the end we managed to salvage him. I hope I can do the same for Craig.'

'You're talking about the man who was dismissed from the hospital where you worked before this, aren't you?'

When he nodded, she said softly, 'I'm sorry that I ever doubted you—over the doctor who was dismissed, over Craig, over all the troubles with my family.' Her eyes clouded. 'They could never come to terms with what your father did, and it's been hard, one way and another, to reconcile everything. I've been pulled all ways, and I needed to be loyal to my family, but I should have believed in you. You weren't to blame for your father's actions.'

'I don't think my dad was wrong in what he did. He made a genuine offer for your father's company, and the shareholders accepted it. What made things difficult was that the board then voted your father out. My dad didn't want that. He protested, but it was a majority vote and he lost. To be fair to him, he stepped down himself after his term of office expired and he left the company. He always regretted what happened to your father, and he tried to explain his actions, but your father refused to hear him out.'

'I'm sorry.' She grimaced. 'It's a mess, isn't it? Two warring families who won't give each other the time of day, and nothing ever seems to change, except that my dad's health is deteriorating little by little.'

'Is he still waiting for treatment?'

She nodded. 'We had to wait until his blood was thinned to avoid the possibility of provoking a stroke, but then he had a setback, and he's still on the waiting list. My mother won't let me see him or talk to him, so I don't know how bad things are right now.' She bit her lip. 'I feel so helpless.'

Drew stroked a hand gently along her arm. 'Don't give up. Give me the name of his specialist and I'll see if I can have a word with him. We might be able to work something out. If he could have a cardioversion to reset the rhythm of his heart, then we can start to sort everything else out. With rest and the right medication, he could be on the road to recovery.'

'I know that. Once he starts to feel better in himself he could get a grip on the business again, and things might begin to look up, but so far I haven't made any headway in getting to see him. My mother is being very protective of him, and she won't let me near.'

His gaze softened, his eyes darkening. 'I'm sorry about that. I always had a lot of respect for your mother, and it's hard to accept that she could behave that way. She must be very worried about him.'

'She is.'

'I'll do what I can to get the specialist to reconsider his case. Leave it with me.'

'Thanks.' By now, Craig was beginning to come round, and Katie heaved a sigh of relief. It had been awful, seeing him like that, and she couldn't imagine how he had let himself get into that state. When he was up to it, she would talk to him and try to get him to see sense.

In the meantime, she turned back to Drew and they headed towards the hospital exit. 'Can I drop you off at home?' Drew asked, but she shook her head.

'I have my car here. Besides, it's best if you stay away for now,' she added flatly. 'Things are bad enough with my family as it is, and if they see you with me it could stir things up again out of all proportion. I want to make my peace with them. I don't want to provoke them any further.'

She looked up at him, hoping for his understanding, but his expression was harsh and uncompromising. A muscle flicked in his jaw. 'If that's the way you want it. I'm sorry that things had to turn out this way. I had hoped things could be different.'

He moved away from her and headed off down the corridor, his brisk strides taking him swiftly away from her.

Katie watched him go, and her stomach felt leaden. She had ruined everything all over again. He didn't appreciate her need to be loyal to her family, and she didn't know how to put things right. She felt sick at heart.

CHAPTER NINE

'I WAS hoping I would find you here. Are you very busy, or can you spare a few minutes to talk?'

Katie glanced up from the lab report she was studying and then opened her eyes wide in surprise. 'Becky?' Her sister-in-law was heavily pregnant, and she looked tired and overheated, her fair hair falling in wispy, faintly damp curls around her face. 'Yes, we can talk. I'm about finished here anyway.'

Katie swiftly looked her over. 'Are you sure you're well enough to be up and about? When did they let you out of hospital?' Katie quickly pulled out a chair and waved a hand towards it. 'Here, come and sit down. You look hot. Can I get you a cold drink to cool you down?'

'Thanks. Yes, I could do with a drink.' Becky did as she had suggested and gingerly lowered herself onto the seat. 'I've been stuck in a traffic jam for half an hour, and it's left me feeling thoroughly frazzled.'

While Becky settled herself in a quiet corner by the desk, Katie hurried away to fetch an iced drink for her. What was she doing here? Whatever the reason, she was a welcome sight. No one from her family had been near her or phoned, and the strain was beginning to drag Katie down.

'Here you are,' Katie murmured, handing her a glass of orange juice. 'That should make you feel better.' She watched Becky take a long swallow, and then said carefully, 'I wanted to come and see you, but the nurses told me I wasn't allowed to. They said you had to rest.'

'I'm sorry about that. It was all Luke's doing, but I didn't know anything about it until they let me go yesterday.' She pressed her lips together in a straight line. 'I'd no idea that he was being so unreasonable, and as soon as I found out what had been going on, I was furious. It's just unbelievable that he should behave that way towards you after all you've done for us.'

'I'm glad that you're talking to me anyway,' Katie said with a relieved smile. 'I was worried that you would be angry with me, too. It's been hard, knowing that I've upset everyone.'

'You certainly haven't upset me. I can't thank you enough for the way you've looked after Reece. He was so unhappy when his father stopped him from seeing you, and I'm absolutely livid with Luke.'

Katie frowned. 'I don't want to be the cause of any trouble between you and Luke. He's had a lot to deal with these last few months. He's had an awful lot to sort out.'

'Well, he's not going about it the right way, is he? Running the business is one thing—he has decisions to make, and sacrifices, and it has certainly been a headache for him—but he can't get away with telling you how to live your life. He has no right to impose his views on you.' Becky studied her. 'How are things with you and Drew through all this? Are they working out all right?'

The direct question took Katie by surprise. 'No, not really,' she said. Sudden tears sprang up in her eyes, and she lowered her head until she had mastered her emotions. 'He's been very withdrawn from me lately. He's never attempted to get involved in the tensions between our two families, and I can't blame him for that, but this constant strife and recrimination is like a wall between us. We can't seem to get over it and reach each other. There's always that barrier, an insurmountable obstacle that neither of us can conquer.'

'I'm so sorry. I wish there was something I could do.'

Katie shook her head. 'You mustn't worry about me. You have enough on your mind with Reece and the baby to prepare for.'

'Even so, I do worry about you.' She frowned. 'Have you spoken to your father about any of this?'

'I haven't. My mother is afraid that I'll make him ill by reminding him of problems he'd rather forget.'

'I'm not so sure about that.' A line creased Becky's brow. 'He came into hospital for his treatment yesterday—did you know?'

Katie was shocked. 'No, I didn't. No one told me.' Even Drew had made no mention of the fact. He had said he would talk to the specialist, but since then he hadn't mentioned it. Had he managed to get things brought forward? Why hadn't he told her what was happening?

'Katie?' Becky's voice pulled her back to reality.

'I'm sorry. I wish I'd known about it.' Anxiously, she studied Becky's face. 'How is he?'

'Last I heard, he was doing well. The shock to the heart put his rhythm back on an even keel, so they should be able to address his other problems now. They're keeping him in hospital for a couple of days for observation and medication, but as far as I know the doctors are pleased with his progress.'

Becky reached out and clasped Katie's hand in hers. 'Why don't you go and see for yourself? Never mind what your mother and Luke say. I think you'll find that he will be glad to talk to you.'

'Do you really think so?'

'I do. If you can get away right now, he'll probably be on his own. Your mother has gone to collect Reece from nursery school for me, and Luke is still at work. Go and see your dad. Talk to him.'

Katie thought about it for a moment, and came to a quick decision. 'I think I will.' She glanced at her watch. 'Thanks, Becky. I'll go and have a word with Drew and see if he'll let me disappear for half an hour or so. Can I help you anywhere or do you want to stay here for a while? Or even come with me?'

Becky shook her head. 'I'll go to the hospital café and get myself a bite to eat before Reece arrives to see his grandad. I can find my own way there. You go and find Drew.'

'I will. Thanks again, Becky.'

Drew was monitoring a patient, but he took time out to listen to her request. 'I didn't realise the cardiologist had brought things forward quite so soon—he said he would take a look at his file and follow up on it, but he didn't get back to me on his decision. I'm pleased that it's all been dealt with and that it went well.' He sent her a swift, searching glance. 'I can understand that you want to see your father, but what if the rest of your family turn up? Are you sure you're ready to deal with all the flak that you might get from them? They may not give you a pleasant reception, given the way they feel towards me.'

'I have to see him.' She made a face. 'I have to at least try to mend fences. They're my flesh and blood after all.'

He looked at her steadily, his eyes giving nothing away. 'That's true. Go and try to make your peace with them. Your shift's due to finish soon anyway. We'll hold the fort down here, but if anything urgent comes in, I'll page you.'

'Thanks.' She sped away, and in a few minutes she was hesitantly opening the door to her father's side room.

He was resting in bed, propped up by pillows, and his eyes were closed as though he was weary. He opened them, though, when he heard her approach.

'Katie?' He appeared startled, and she approached him tentatively.

'I didn't know that you were here until a few minutes ago,' she said.

'No.' He looked down at the bed sheet, and she thought he was about to say something more, but then he stopped himself and simply gazed at her.

Awkwardly, she said, 'How are you? How did the treatment go?'

'It went well…better than they expected, I think. It was all a bit of a rush in the end. One day I received the phone call, and the next I was in here, being checked out for the anaesthetic.'

She slid into a chair by the bedside. 'And do you feel all right?'

He nodded. 'I'm very tired, but I'm feeling much better than I did. The doctors say it will take time.' He didn't say any more and Katie floundered, not used to this hesitant, guarded relationship. It was awful, talking to her father in such a tentative fashion, feeling like a stranger, fraught and uncomfortable.

She said uneasily, 'Dad, I'm sorry if I've disappointed you or hurt you in any way. I wish things could have been different because I wouldn't want to upset you for the world.'

'In what way do you think you've disappointed me?'

'By my relationship with Drew…by not being a son who could carry on the business in your place…'

Just then the door opened and her mother walked into the room with Luke. They stared at her but said nothing, just frowned, and immediately she felt like

an outcast once more, rejected and forlorn. Then
Reece appeared from behind his father, gave a little
whoop of joy and ran over to her. He flung his arms
around her and she hugged him in return.

'Look what I got, Auntie Katie. I got a windmill
flower, and it goes round and round when you blow
on it. See…' He demonstrated, and the plastic flower
whirled in myriad colours. 'It's for Grandad. It's to
make him happy, so he gets better fast.'

'I'm sure he'll love it,' Katie said with a strained
little smile. 'Why don't you go and give it to him?'

'I will.' He rushed over to the bed and presented it
to his grandad, who admired it as though it were the
most precious gift in the world.

Katie's mother looked across at her, a worried expression in her eyes, as though she was afraid Katie
being there would upset her father. Luke stared, his
mouth straight, as if he was struggling to keep in his
thoughts. Perhaps he was cautious of saying what he
felt in front of Reece.

A moment later there was a knock at the door, and
then it was pushed open and Drew stood there, not
coming into the room but sending a swift glance
around, as though checking that all was well.

'Sorry to interrupt,' he said, and then glanced at
Katie. 'I thought you should know—do you remember the little boy you treated some time ago? The one
who kept fainting, and you diagnosed his heart problem?'

She nodded. 'Yes, I remember.'

'Well, he's coming in to see you in a little while—in around fifteen minutes or so. Apparently he's doing very well now, and he wants to say thank you. His mother wanted to know if you would be able to see him. I told her I was sure you would want to. Was I right?'

She smiled. 'Yes, of course.'

'Good.' He glanced around once more. No one spoke. They returned his stare, and it was as though they were frozen to the spot, except for Reece, who was intent on blowing the windmill into a rainbow of colour, oblivious to the tensions all around him.

Drew made a brief, tight smile. 'I'll leave you to it, then. Sorry for the intrusion.'

Katie was suddenly galvanised into action. 'No, wait. Don't go, Drew.' She stood up. 'I want to thank you for all you've done, for arranging everything with the specialist, for making sure this could happen…and for being so patient when everyone was against you.' She went over to him and touched his arm. 'I should never have doubted you or tried to deny the way I feel about you. You deserve better than that. Can you forgive me for the way I've treated you?'

She looked into his eyes, and suddenly they were as deep as the ocean, and she was being pulled into their depths, but instead of drowning and struggling against the tide, she was buoyed up by the warmth and compassion she saw there.

He cupped her hand in his. 'There's nothing to forgive. I'm just glad that I could be there for you. I told you, you only have to ask.'

She turned away from him and faced her family. 'I didn't ever want to upset any of you, you need to know that. You're my flesh and blood, and I love you all deeply, and I hate to think that you feel you have to push me away, but I love Drew and I need to acknowledge that to the world. If you can't accept that, then I'm truly sorry, but I can't go on denying the truth. You all have to move on and face the future, not the past. My future is with Drew. I really hope you can all come round to accepting that because I want you to be part of my life, too.'

Drew gently squeezed her hand and she swung around to face him once more. His mouth was curved in a faint smile, and he said softly, 'I'm glad that you finally managed to sort out your feelings. I've been out in the wilderness for so long that I was beginning to feel cold and lonely. It's good to have you back.'

Suddenly everyone was talking at once. Her mother said, 'Katie, we didn't mean to push you away. I was just so worried about your dad, and I know I went too far. I'm so sorry. You know I want you to be happy, but I just couldn't see beyond your father's illness.'

Luke was frowning heavily. 'I shouldn't have treated you the way I did. Becky made me see that. All I can say is that I think I felt overwhelmed by the pressure I was under, and I needed to find someone I could blame. You were the nearest one to hand, and

I took my frustration out on you. I should never have let things get to that stage.'

'It's all right.' Katie looked from one to the other. 'Just as long as you recognize that Drew has a place in my life, too. That's all I ask.'

She was overwhelmed by the way things had turned around. She had thought she had lost her family, but now it looked as though all that had changed, and she knew that this was a lesson they would all take to heart.

She cast a worried glance across the room at her father. Would all this upset have made him ill?

He sent her a smile in return, and she went over to him and stroked his hand. 'Are you all right? I hope I haven't made you ill in any way.'

'You know, Katie, you startled me with what you said earlier. You have never been a disappointment to me.' He gripped her hand warmly. 'I've always been proud of you, and I've always wanted only the very best for you. I'm proud that you chose to be a doctor rather than follow me into the family business.' He winced. 'I'm sorry if I made you feel uncomfortable about being with Drew. You have my blessing. I've been selfish, and that is going to change from now on.'

He looked at Luke and said quietly, 'I placed too great a burden on your shoulders, and I'm proud of the way you kept things going while I was ill. Things are going to be different from now on. Once I'm out of here I'm going to recruit a young graduate trainee to eventually take over the administrative side of things, and you can go back to doing what you do best…design work. We've some orders coming in because I tried what Katie suggested some time ago, giving clients a trial period to see if they liked the product. It's beginning to pay dividends now, and things should start to improve.'

He glanced from son to daughter. 'I'm proud of both of you.' His gaze went to Drew. 'I understand I have you to thank for bringing my treatment forward. The cardiologist told me that you had spoken to him. I'm very grateful for what you did, and I don't know how to make amends for the way we've treated you.'

'You could try talking to my father,' Drew said. 'He always regretted what happened, and he wanted more than anything to put things right. He probably knows of some bright young graduates who would be only too glad to work with you and help you sort things out. Why don't you give him a call?'

'Perhaps I will. Just as soon as I'm out of hospital.' Her father smiled. 'I've had time to think things through these last few days, and reflect on why all this has come about. For a long time I was angry and disillusioned, and I felt that all my work had gone to waste. I think I was wrong. My health has been poor these last few years, and it coloured my judgement and made me sour. I'm sorry for that, for the way it made me behave, and I hope I can start to put things right. Like Katie says, we have to look to the future, not dwell in the past.'

'I'm glad to hear you say it.' Drew glanced at Katie. 'I've loved Katie for as long as I can remember, and I want her to be happy. I've hated seeing her under all this strain.'

Katie reached out and touched his arm in a gesture of love and affection, and he covered her hand with his. 'I don't like to drag you away,' he murmured, 'but I expect young Sam Slater will be here in a few minutes. Shall we go down and say hello?'

She nodded, and they left the room together. His clasp was warm and firm, and for the first time in ages she felt safe and secure, and at peace with herself.

Sam arrived in A and E a minute or so after Katie and Drew got there, and shyly planted a kiss on Katie's cheek.

'I bought you some flowers,' he said, 'to say thank you for listening to me and for looking after me. I feel ever so much better now.'

'I'm really glad, Sam,' Katie told him. 'You look well. You go on taking care of yourself, and come and see me again if you like.'

'I will.'

He left a few minutes later with his mother, and Drew said quietly, 'Our shift ended a while ago. Do you want to go back up to your father's room? You didn't get much time to talk and sort things out.'

'Yes. That's a good idea.'

They walked back towards the side ward, and Katie sent Drew a sideways glance. Throughout all this he had been so calm and strong, never standing in the way of what she had wanted to do. How could she have been so blind as to ignore the glaringly obvious? She loved him. She had always loved him, and she would never be happy without him by her side.

'What are you thinking?' He sent her a quizzical look.

'That I love you, and I've been incredibly foolish to almost let you slip away.'

'I would never have slipped away.'

'Wouldn't you?'

'Never.' He drew her into a kitchen area, shielded from prying eyes. 'I've always known that you were the only woman for me. I just needed you to discover that I was the only man for you.'

She looked at him, wide-eyed. 'You never told me that before.'

'You were young—too young—and I didn't want to stand in your way. You had your whole life ahead of you, and you were setting out on your career. Then this business with my father happened and I didn't know how to play it. I wanted to tell you that I couldn't let you go, but that would have meant alienating you from your family, and then you might have grown to hate me. I had to let you find your own way to me.'

She lifted her arms up around his neck. 'I love you so much. I've wasted so much time. Can you ever forgive me?'

He kissed her gently on the mouth. 'Only if you

agree that you owe me. You have to promise to kiss me twice for every day that's passed since we first met.'

She smiled into his eyes. 'That's a debt that's going to take for ever to pay.'

'Yes, I imagine it will.' He lowered his head and kissed her soundly, and she arched her body against him until he pressed her back against the kitchen wall and folded her in his arms. Her soft feminine curves melted into the hard male strength of his body.

Coming up for breath a few minutes later, she said huskily, 'You make my head whirl. I feel as though I'm intoxicated.'

'I'm glad about that.' He kissed her again. 'Will you marry me?'

'Yes, please…make it soon.'

'As soon as we can arrange it.' He ran his thumb gently over her cheek, delicately tracing the outline of her face. 'You know I bought the house for you, don't you?'

'Did you?'

He nodded soberly. 'You belong there. With me.'

He kissed her once more, and a small voice piped up from the doorway, 'Are you two getting married?'

Katie turned and saw Reece. 'Yes, we are.'

'Can I come?'

'I wouldn't get married without you being there. You can be my page boy if you like.'

He screwed up his nose at that. 'What's a page boy?'

'He's someone who helps a bride at her wedding. She walks down the aisle at the church, and she wears a lovely dress—perhaps with a train flowing behind it—and she holds some beautiful flowers, and she might need a bit of help. So she has page boys and bridesmaids to be her helpers.'

'And I can do that?'

'Yes.'

He sent her a beaming smile. 'I'm going to tell my mummy.' He ran out of the kitchen, and they heard him run into her father's room next door, saying eagerly, 'I'm going to a wedding. The bride needs someone to turn her pages in her book, so I'm going to do it. Katie can't do it herself because she has to hold her flowers and all that, and she might fall over when she gets on the train if she doesn't look where she's going. Then Drew would have to pick her up and kiss her all over again.' His voice lowered conspiratorially. 'They keep doing that. Kissing.' He gave an exaggerated sigh. 'I don't know why. It's silly if you ask me.'

Kate and Drew looked at each other and laughed. Drew said, 'We'd better go and tell them what's going on before he ad-libs any more. We don't want to confuse them any more than we have to, do we?'

He bent his head and kissed her firmly on the mouth. 'I love you, Katie. Promise me that you'll keep that at the forefront of your mind. I'll always love you.'

'I promise,' she whispered. 'I love you.'

MILLS & BOON® 0605/03b

Live the emotion

_Medical
romance™

A SPECIAL KIND OF CARING by Jennifer Taylor

Dr Francesca Goodwin wants to escape – from
London, from the pain of her last relationship, from
people. Working as a GP in isolated Teesdale sounds
perfect – until she meets her new partner, Dr Alex
Shepherd. He's good-looking, caring – and attracted
to her!

THE FLIGHT DOCTOR'S LIFELINE by Laura Iding

(Air Rescue)

Helicopter pilot Reese Jarvis is drawn to Dr Samantha
Kearn from the moment he sees her in action with the
Lifeline Medical Air Transport team. When he learns
she is having trouble with her ex-husband, he
immediately wants to protect her. He becomes her
lifeline, her support – but ever since his fiancée died he
has been reluctant to put his feelings on the line…

THE BUSH DOCTOR'S RESCUE by Leah Martyn

Nurse Ally Inglis doesn't know why Dr Marc Ballantyne
has come to the Outback town of Hillcrest, she's just
grateful to have a full-time doctor at last. Marc charms
and surprises everyone – not least of all Ally. He stirs
up feelings she thought she'd never have again. But she
can't help wondering, does this modern-day knight *really*
mean to rescue her heart…?

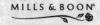

FREE!

4 Books
and a surprise gift!

We would like to take this opportunity to thank you for reading this Mills & Boon® book by offering you the chance to take FOUR more specially selected titles from the Medical Romance™ series absolutely FREE! We're also making this offer to introduce you to the benefits of the Reader Service™—

- ★ **FREE home delivery**
- ★ **FREE gifts and competitions**
- ★ **FREE monthly Newsletter**
- ★ **Exclusive Reader Service offers**
- ★ **Books available before they're in the shops**

Accepting these FREE books and gift places you under no obligation to buy, you may cancel at any time, even after receiving your free shipment. Simply complete your details below and return the entire page to the address below. You don't even need a stamp!

YES! Please send me 4 free Medical Romance books and a surprise gift. I understand that unless you hear from me, I will receive 6 superb new titles every month for just £2.75 each, postage and packing free. I am under no obligation to purchase any books and may cancel my subscription at any time. The free books and gift will be mine to keep in any case.

M5ZEF

Ms/Mrs/Miss/Mr ....Initials ....
BLOCK CAPITALS PLEASE

Surname ....

Address ....

....

....Postcode ....../...........

Send this whole page to:
UK: FREEPOST CN81, Croydon, CR9 3WZ

Offer valid in UK only and is not available to current Reader service subscribers to this series. Overseas and Eire please write for details. We reserve the right to refuse an application and applicants must be aged 18 years or over. Only one application per household. Terms and prices subject to change without notice. Offer expires 30th September 2005. As a result of this application, you may receive offers from Harlequin Mills & Boon and other carefully selected companies. If you would prefer not to share in this opportunity please write to The Data Manager, PO Box 676, Richmond, TW9 IWU.

Mills & Boon® is a registered trademark owned by Harlequin Mills & Boon Limited.
Medical Romance™ is being used as a trademark. The Reader Service™ is being used as a trademark.